The Diary on the FIFTH FLOOR

Raisha Lalwani, a reader by day and a writer by night, is a content homemaker. Her passion for writing started at an early age and has been growing since.

After being trained as a singer in Hindustani classical music and having graduated from Delhi University, she got her master's degree in International Business.

Having lived in Mumbai, Jaipur, Delhi and Dubai, Raisha is well-travelled, with exposure to different cities and cultures. Her need to pen things down has resulted in her debut novel, *The Diary on the Fifth Floor*. A fine line between fact and fiction, the book is a collection of short hard-hitting stories in the form of diary entries.

Praise for the Book

Raisha has made a stunning entrance into the literary world. The pen has just found a beautiful new purpose.

—SONAM K AHUJA

Raisha has used a very unconventional style of writing that is brave, fresh and straight from the heart. Her first book is a riveting read. She takes on a host of societal issues, exposing the darker side of human behaviour with an inherent passion. In crisp and concise language, *The Diary on the Fifth Floor* evokes strong emotions. A must read!

—SOHA ALI KHAN

They say a picture is worth a thousand words. But every word in this book conjures up a perfect picture of the author's inner thoughts and emotions. For her very unique story concept and narrative, Raisha is to be congratulated. This is a great effort for a debut book.

—PRABHU CHAWLA
(Editorial Director, The New Indian Express group)

This is a remarkably gripping book about our everyday life, its trials and travails. What emerges from this struggle is the indestructible human energy which makes us search for a purpose in life that is so challenging. Sensitively written, this set of short stories is a page-turner.

—CHANDAN MITRA
(Former Bharatiya Janata Party MP and Editor, The Pioneer)

The Diary on the FIFTH FLOOR

RAISHA LALWANI

RUPA

Published by
Rupa Publications India Pvt. Ltd 2018
7/16, Ansari Road, Daryaganj
New Delhi 110002

Sales centres:
Allahabad Bengaluru Chennai
Hyderabad Jaipur Kathmandu
Kolkata Mumbai

ISBN: 978-93-5304-935-5

Second impression 2019

10 9 8 7 6 5 4 3 2

Printed at Repro Knowledge Cast Limited, Mumbai

For My Dad

'It's what life is, it's a series of rooms, and who we get stuck in those rooms with, adds up to what our lives are.'

—House, MD

Contents

PROLOGUE

Look around and observe...

You wouldn't be able to point out even five things that could be considered truly genuine.

Think about it.

On Monday,

The water you used to brush your teeth was contaminated by the minute.

The cup of tea you began your morning with had water and food colouring, not milk.

The spices in your food contained fertilizers.

The cardigan you wore was not a 100 per cent wool.

The doors you walked through did not have solid locks. They were replaced with cheap ones by the locksmiths, so that you could call them every now and then for repairs.

Your kids were at school; the younger ones still in bliss, playing the day away in utter delight. The elder one, however, was really confused as to which car would be at the front gate after school to pick him up. Would it be the new Audi? The Porsche? After all, the name of the car is directly related to the number of 'friends' he is going to make this year.

That evening, you got home after a long, exhausting day, only to be welcomed by the warmth of recently microwaved food. What did you do then? You put on the same old smile. It might have been faint, but at least it was there.

There was barely enough energy to eat the food, let alone argue about it. You went to bed, hoping to spend time with the spouse; but he'd had an equally exhausting day. And so, you both pretended to be asleep.

Tuesday...

Wednesday...

Thursday...

Friday...

Rewind, replay.

You want to start over?

Rewind.

But this time, pause before you hit the play button.

The choices we make define the kind
Of people we then become.

The main question here is:
Do we like who we have become?

Chapter One

OH, TO BE A CHILD AGAIN

As a child, I would spend at least fifteen minutes every other morning before going to school, trying to convince my parents that I was feeling unwell. My parents, however, were not so easy to fool. Whether my excuse was a stomach ache, a headache, a cramp in the leg or even simple nausea, my mother would know that it was all a big lie. And yet, I tried, every morning. Kids today, they have it easy. All they have to do is mention that the car window had been open on the way home from school, and that the road had been filled with trucks—these days, this would be a valid enough reason for a parent to think twice.

Pollution. Choking, blinding, billowing pollution, filling the city and our lungs.

It is beyond doubt that there are hundreds of advantages of living in a big city. The number one reason, of course, being that cities are big in every sense. There are more opportunities, more people to socialize with, better deals to be found in the market—not to mention twenty-four hour coffee shops, twenty-four hour airports, better healthcare, better education...one could go on at length about it. But, the immediate drawback is that so many people also mean so much more traffic—and that can drive anyone crazy.

On this particular morning, we were moving so slow that I could have walked and still reached ahead of my car. Outside the window was the same sight as seen every single day. A swarm of cars in every direction, angry at each other, angry at the world, destroying any chance a hapless pedestrian had at walking on the road. Rumbling engines, unnecessary smoke, meaningless honks coming from all directions and yet no progression.

'Stop! Stop!' I said.

As the driver slowed down the car to a standstill near the pavement, I looked up at the signboard once more. There it was—*Holy Grace Hospital*—staring at me in big grey letters.

'It's okay,' I said to my driver as I got out of the car. 'I'll walk from here.'

He was quick to follow me out of the car, and closed the door behind me. 'Madam, is it okay if I park the car in the service lane? This road gets really busy at this time of the day.'

I had reached the hospital after hours of being held captive by the traffic in my own car, and where the car was going to be parked was the least of my concerns. The appointment I had arrived for was everything—I just had to meet this doctor. I had been trying to get a meeting with her for weeks, and after countless emails and phone calls she had finally agreed to see me. There was no way I was going to arrive late for this appointment.

'That's all right,' I said shortly. 'I'll call you once I'm done here.'

I crossed the road and power-walked my way into the hospital building.

In general, hospitals make me nauseous. It's the smell of the disinfectant that makes me uncomfortable and queasy, which is why my first question to the doctor's assistant, a few days ago, had been if I could see the doctor at her clinic instead of at the hospital. That had not been possible and so, I stood outside the glass door for a moment, steeling myself to brave the smell. Beyond the door, a housekeeping guy was aimlessly mopping the floor, most likely adding to the ever-present odour of cleaning solutions. I took a long, deep breath, covered my mouth and nose with my scarf, and opened the door.

As I walked in, I kept looking back. Never in my life had I been so conscious of my presence at a place. I could see a huge pharmacy on my left, crowded with people getting their prescriptions filled. Across the pharmacy was the reception. I walked in that direction, and joined the queue.

Several minutes later, I found myself standing face-to-face with a man seated in a chair on the other side of the glass partition. It was hard to tell if he was feeling tired, or was lazy, or simply had no interest in his appearance. His posture was far from being ideal, his hair was unkempt, and there was a frown on his face.

Looking up, he asked, 'How can I help you?'

'Dr Rama Berry?' I asked.

He looked at me in a way we look at the hand towel in a public washroom. After what seemed like the longest pause, he replied, 'Fifth floor.'

Turning away from him irritably, I started to walk towards the elevators that ran along one wall.

'Hold it!' I shouted from a distance at the man who was getting into the elevator marked 'Visitors Only'. I ran towards it and stumbled to see that there was hardly any space. Nonetheless, I managed to squeeze myself in. With his finger poised over the buttons, the man who had held the lift open for me asked, 'Which floor?'

'Fifth,' I replied.

A few moments later, the elevator door opened, revealing a board that read: 'Fifth Floor: Psychiatric Ward'. I stepped out of the elevator, and following the directions on the board, turned right into a corridor. After walking through what felt like an endless passage, I found myself standing outside the doctor's door.

Dr Rama Berry

MBBS, MD (Psychiatry)

I realized it was time to let go of the half-damp tissue I had been crushing and squeezing ever since I had entered the hospital. I quickly threw it in the bin, finger brushed my hair, straightened my clothes and knocked. A moment later, a woman opened the door and ushered me in.

The room was nothing like I had imagined it might look. To begin with, it didn't look like a part of this hospital—or any other hospital, for that matter. The room was well-lit and well-ventilated. The curtains were a vibrant shade of yellow, and the wallpaper was fresh green with a leaf-like print on it. The extreme corner on the left had a huge bookshelf. I flicked my glance to read the spines of the books and realized they were mostly based on positive thinking, healing, achieving, etc.

There were all kinds of potted plants; fake or real, I couldn't tell. Best of all, the 'hospital smell' was gone, instead, there was a familiar and comforting fragrance filling the air. It was as if I had entered a spa; I immediately felt calmer; I think the smell might have been lavender. I felt suddenly better, somehow reassured that I had come to the right place, and more importantly, was about to meet the right person.

'I have an appointment,' I told one of Dr Berry's assistants, stepping-up to the desk she stood behind. 'Yes, yes…' she muttered, before handing me a form. 'Just fill this out.'

Lifting a pen from the holder on the table, I looked at the sheet of paper. It was a short questionnaire—contact information, primarily—but the first question already made me pause. I had to be careful, or the whole thing would fall apart.

Name—the question seemed to mock me.

Skipping that one, I filled in the answers to all the other questions on the form, before returning to the first.

I filled in the blanks—Sairah Khanna, and handed it back to Dr Berry's assistant.

The woman's eyes scanned the form quickly, before returning to mine, filled with surprise.

'You are here for the appointment at 4.30 p.m.; is that right, madam?' she asked.

'Yes,' I replied firmly.

'But, I have the patient's name in my appointment record as Savannah Khanna?'

'No, that's right,' I clarified, wishing I had lied on the form. I could have told the doctor the truth, if it came to that. 'That's who I am here for. Savannah. She's my...'

'What?' asked the assistant, before I could finish. 'That's not... I'm not sure you understand how this works, Madam!'

Before she could continue, however, the intercom on her table began to ring. She used the speakerphone to answer.

'Is the patient here? Send her in,' announced a female voice. It was a strong, confident voice, brooking no opposition.

And so, ignoring the assistant's puzzled look, I walked into Dr Rama Berry's office.

Chapter Two

THE APPOINTMENT

'It seems that I am the last one for the day.'

My tone was light as I greeted Dr Berry while walking into her room, but I was a little shaken by what had just happened. What if Dr Berry refused to take on the case? Could I tell her everything?

My mind was preoccupied with myriad thoughts, while my eyes scanned the room. It was tastefully decorated, and by the number of awards and degrees that had been framed and hung on one of the walls, its owner was a person of some achievement. There was a long comfortable-looking tan-coloured couch on the right side of the desk and an old yet beautifully-carved rocking chair by the window.

Dr Berry herself was a small, almost diminutive woman, with a shock of white hair that cascaded down her back. She was dressed in a simple yet tasteful sari, and an engraved bangle of gold gleamed discreetly from one forearm.

'Yes, you are,' she smiled, stepping around her desk and welcoming me into the room. 'Come in, please. Come, take a seat. I don't believe we have met before, have we?'

As I took a seat on that comfortable sofa, I tried to compose an answer to her inevitable question. What am I going to tell her? I should never have come! As I worried, the assistant who had taken my form, stepped into the room and handed Dr Berry a white file with my name—Sairah—written in bold black letters on the front. The woman then left, giving me a confused smile; and as the door clicked closed, Dr Berry spoke again.

'Sairah?' smiled the doctor, looking up from the file a moment later. She had taken a seat near me before opening the file, hiding nothing from me; in the file was a single sheet of paper, with my name and contact information on it, along with a note written in blue ink. 'Ah, there's a note…' she paused, and then looked up once more. 'It says you're here on someone else's behalf? Is that right, my dear? A lady, I presume, named Savannah Khanna?'

Dr Berry had a warm, unassuming manner, and laughter crinkled in the corners of her eyes, and it was then that I realized why she was one of the city's best psychiatrists.

'Yes, doctor,' I replied meekly, feeling a little more at ease. The assistant, on the other hand, had been so brusque and sure of herself.

'That is either highly unusual or possibly, quite understandable, my dear,' Dr Berry said with a comforting laugh. She then fell silent, waiting for my response.

'Ah...yes, doctor,' I managed. 'I came on behalf of Savannah, my...my sister. She said she didn't want people to think she was...' I fell silent.

Dr Berry surprised me then by laughing again, more warmly this time. 'That is quite normal my dear,' she said calmly, patting me on the hand. 'It is quite common for people to be nervous or embarrassed about visiting a psychiatrist. It shouldn't be, but it is. May I presume that your sister asked you to contact me on her behalf?'

'Not...not exactly,' I replied, my mouth going dry. I fell silent.

Noticing my discomfort, Dr Berry spoke once more, and her words immediately calmed me again. 'You must care greatly for your sister, my dear. Tell me, Sairah, are you always this persistent or is it just in this case?'

I smiled despite my unease—Dr Berry was, no doubt, referring to the many emails I had sent her over the past few days. Two weeks ago, her office had informed me that the waiting list to see Dr Berry was several months long, and there was absolutely no way of making an exception for me. It was then that I had begun emailing Dr Berry herself, at first hesitantly, and then, in a flood. I had first read her name in a health magazine; she had been featured as the *'Shining*

Star of Medicine' of the country. From that moment, I had a feeling that Dr Berry was the only person who could help me.

'I'm so sorry, doctor. I know how much I have troubled you, but I really wanted to see you, and I appreciate this opportunity...'

'You are quite welcome, my dear,' replied the doctor warmly. 'I could see from your emails that your concern was genuine, though I now understand why you were so guarded when I asked you for details. Now that you are here, however, I must tell you that I cannot possibly help your sister if she does not wish to see me. I can understand that you, as her sister...'

'But doctor, you don't understand,' I burst in, not caring how rude I was being by interrupting. 'You have to help... her! Savannah needs your help!'

'I don't mean to disappoint you my dear, but you have to understand, I can't really be of much help to her unless I can meet her or talk to her.'

I was silent, and Dr Berry could see the indecision on my face.

'There are things I would need to know,' she continued gently. 'Things only your sister could possibly know. Matters that she may be confused about. Patterns of thought or behaviour that she may not even be aware of. You see?' Her smile was as gentle as before.

'I'm her sister!' I tried again. 'I grew up with... I know

her, doctor! Better than she knows herself, sometimes! I could tell you everything you need to...'

But, Dr Berry was shaking her head, her expression growing firm. 'I'm sorry, my dear,' she said. 'It would be dangerous, and perhaps even immoral for a psychiatrist to treat a patient in such a manner. Certainly not...unless, you had an immediate fear for your sister's life?'

'No,' I shook my head, my gaze falling to the floor. There was a leaden feeling in the pit of my stomach, and though I was well in control of it, I could feel the now-familiar urge to just give in and cry. Why does it all have to be so difficult? I thought despairingly. What am I going to do now?

I looked up, trying to shake off the feeling of dejection. Dr Berry was looking directly at me, into my eyes, and despite the bitter sadness that was overwhelming me, I couldn't help but notice the kindness shining out of her eyes. There was so much wisdom, and confidence and clarity in the way she spoke. Her hair neatly parted, though allowed to cascade freely down her back, her sari properly pinned up. She was calm and composed, just as a doctor should be.

'Well, at the very least,' she said briskly, 'since you have made the effort of coming all the way here, perhaps I can offer a bit of advice. The only reason I agreed to see you—you must understand, I do not often make exceptions to my rule of following the order of patients—is because...' she hesitated. When she spoke again, it was as though she was inching her way forward on to a thin plank. 'There was a great deal of sorrow in those letters, my dear. As though the one who wrote it was asking for help herself.'

Chapter Three

TRUTH BE TOLD

My mouth was completely dry—I had not counted on Dr Berry being that intuitive. Feeling helpless, I was quiet for a few long moments, and then I spoke, barely holding back my tears.

'Savannah... she is my sister. She was once... once so full of life. She was so... so alive, and had such a good vibe... even strangers would want to come up and talk to her. When she smiled, her face would light up, and she had a way of speaking that left people both impressed and inspired.'

I hesitated.

Dr Berry only nodded, her calm features giving nothing away.

'Maybe she truly was like that,' I said, my voice sounding brittle as I forced the sadness away, 'or maybe it was just me.

She…she is my sister, after all. My best friend.' Dr Berry nodded.

'But, she needs your help, doctor,' I managed with a weak smile, and suddenly the dam burst. The tears began to flow, and I buried my face in my hands and wept.

When the tears had passed, my throat felt raw and my heart was heavy.

'I am here to help,' Dr Berry's voice was as calm as it had been a few moments ago. She offered me a quick smile, before her face relaxed once more into composure. 'It may sound silly, but please, do not worry. You are not alone.'

I nodded, smiling weakly. 'I'm sorry, doctor. The strain of…'

'I understand,' she said gently. 'Tell me about Savannah. When did you notice the change in her behaviour? In what ways has she changed?'

'It's been a few months, now,' I said softly, the tears mostly gone. I felt drained, but the doctor sitting in front of me seemed to exude a glow of peacefulness. Her eyes were filled with sympathy, but otherwise, her expression was one of absolute peace. 'For the last few months, Savannah has not been herself, doctor.'

'Has this happened before?' she asked. 'Her moods abruptly changing?'

'I… I don't know, doctor,' I replied in confusion. I'd truly never given much thought to something like that, but just then, I would have clung to anything that offered hope. 'Why? Is there a cure for... whatever it is that Savannah has?'

'It's autumn now,' Dr Berry waved a hand towards the large windows that lined one wall, overlooking a well-watered garden pocket with a number of spindly trees. 'The season affects people in many different ways; we always see a spike in the number of cases of depression around this time of the year.'

'I...' I shook my head, not convinced. It sounded wrong. If anything, it was too simple an explanation.

'I don't think that's the reason, doctor. She doesn't talk to anyone, doesn't like to meet anyone. She used to love tasting different cuisines, but now she's lost her appetite. She must have lost eight kilos in the past two months alone! Her face looks tired all the time, as though she doesn't sleep. She's... she's just become someone else!'

'Someone else?' I could see Dr Berry scribbling a few quick notes on a pad of crisp paper. Her movements were assured and quick, and from her calm, unhurried demeanour, I found the strength to go on.

'Her mother is not in the country, so she has been staying with her... with our grandparents for the past few months,' I continued distractedly, thinking about the last month. 'Two weeks ago, granny told me that even she was worried! Savvy always kept her room spic and span—fresh sheets, a clean bathroom, her clothes washed and dry-cleaned. And now it's like…she doesn't shower for days! Her room is always a mess. It seems as though she's lost interest in everything.'

'When you wrote to me, you said her age was 25?' Dr Berry prodded gently.

I nodded gratefully. 'Exactly!' I said. 'You have to believe me when I say that it's very out of character for her to behave like this! Sometimes, she just sits by herself, staring blankly for hours on end. It's difficult to tell whether she is even living in the same world as everyone else. I've been staying in with her for days now because she doesn't wish to leave the house. And even when I do manage to get her to smile, it's not the same, doctor.'

Though the tears had begun once again, I felt slightly better. It truly did feel like a weight was being lifted off my chest.

'Her smile is not the same?'

'It's there, but it's vacant!'

'I see,' she nodded contemplatively. 'Tell me something, Sairah. Has Savannah experienced any loss lately? A death? A romantic or a financial loss?'

'Savvy…we lost our dad when she was very young, but she didn't let anyone see that she was upset about it. I caught her wiping away her tears sometimes, but she would soon be her cheery self again. In fact, mom still talks about how supportive Savvy was throughout. Other than that…I can't think of any recent loss. But…but, she has been working on a piece for the last few months, and since then…yes, that is when I started noticing a change in her behaviour.'

'A "piece", you say?' asked the doctor. 'What kind of piece?'

'A book, doctor,' I replied quickly. 'A piece of writing. She said she wanted to write a book.'

'A book? At the age of twenty-five? That's impressive!' Dr Berry smiled, encouragingly.

I nodded, my mood perking up. 'I think it was about… five months ago. We had gone to the Public Library to get our memberships renewed. After our work was done, we decided to sit down for a while. I was in the corner on the far left, looking at the textbooks I would soon need, and she was at the other end where the non-fiction section was. I had a lot of research to do, so I asked her not to wait for me and to leave for home. I didn't give it any thought, but I found her there three hours later, still reading something. That's when she told me: "I think I should write."'

'About what?' asked the doctor.

'She wouldn't say.'

'I see,' said Dr Berry, nodding to herself and picking up her pad. She seemed to be weighing something in her mind, and for a moment, she gazed into nothing; her eyes staring blindly at a large painting of a lighthouse overlooking the sea that hung on the wall near the door.

I could feel a rush of hope; there was something about

Dr Berry's assured manner that convinced me that everything was going to be okay. And best of all, I would never have to tell her about the lie. Feeling a little at ease, I turned to my handbag, opened it, and began to search inside.

'Actually,' my voice had grown relaxed, 'I have something that might help. You see,' I paused guiltily, thinking should I tell another small lie? But, I finally concluded that it's worth it. 'I had gone to see Savvy this morning—I thought I might be able to convince her to come see you, but when I realized it was not going to work, I waited for her to leave the room and quietly took this out from her dresser drawer.'

The book I finally fished out of my bag was a slim notebook, bound in blue cloth. It had a single word written on the cover, in red ink that had become purple because of the cloth—'Diary'.

'In fact, I'm quite certain she must have noticed by now that it is missing,' I continued, the rush of telling the lie kept me talking. 'But I couldn't help it, doctor! Today was my only chance to see you, and I want to help you, help her!'

I put the book down on the long table of polished wood that sat in front of the sofa, and slid the slim book towards Dr Berry. She no longer looked thoughtful. Now, all her attention was on me, ignoring the book entirely.

'It's her diary, doctor! This is Savannah Khanna on paper!'

Dr Berry was silent for a long moment, before she stood

up and slowly bent to pick up the diary. She then began walking towards a broad table that stood near one of the windows, which was piled thickly with sheets of paper.

'I will take up the case, my dear,' her tone was contemplative, 'and if you agree, I will see you here two weeks from today, once again at 4.30 p.m.; but I have one condition.'

'What is that?'

'That you agree to end this deception once and for all and admit that you are Savannah Khanna. Sairah Khanna does not even exist, does she?'

Her tone brooked no opposition, as though she were stating a simple fact. There was not the slightest hint of hesitation or uncertainty in Dr Berry's voice or manner.

Savannah felt a sullen anger rising, a resentment that came from her elaborate secret. I could deny that outright and then walk out of here, she thought. I don't need to take this from...from some stranger! How dare she!

But, there was something about the calm certainty with which Dr Berry was now watching her—a gaze that was interested, compassionate, and above all, absolutely lacking in judgement of any kind—that made her pause.

'What makes you say that I'm not...'

'Many reasons, my dear.'

'Like what?'

'Well, the way you spoke of "her" mother but "your" grandparents; the manner in which you hesitate whenever you begin a sentence about your sister. But mostly, my dear, because you made a simple mistake.'

'Mistake? What mistake?'

'In the form that you filled for my assistant, my dear,' Dr Berry sounded a bit apologetic, 'under "Siblings", you wrote "None".'

Chapter Four

SAVANNAH KHANNA'S DIARY

I am hurt.

The world has given me reasons to be.

Perhaps I should write down everything that is happening...

I should.

I should write a book.

~

All of us have stories,

In our lives, in our hearts. But is anyone listening?

One has to be inspired to write.

I found mine listening to people.

I could feel their pain,

I could connect.

People need to know their words hurt.
They need to know their actions have consequences.
It's hard to begin when you are not sure,
When and how it all began.
But I have promised to be honest
And so, I will try.

~

Book title options:

- Emotions Gone Practical
- Humans—The Tainted Species

Subject of the book:

- The society we live in
- An experience of my neighbour
- Experiences I have been through
- The incident that happened to a friend
- On the people we meet everyday
- Something I witnessed

Remember to keep it clean
Remember to keep it real.
Should I name names, or change them?

~

This happened today.

I don't know what to think, so I am writing about it.

RIP Granny

At first, the sound was soothing.

Like the sound of church bells ringing at a distance, or maybe the kind of music that comes from the waves in the sea. As if it were a dream; one with a background score.

It was wind chimes, perhaps; but I could hear them loud and clear, getting even louder by the moment.

Quickly, the sound became loud enough to be jarring.

I tried hard to shake it off but it just wouldn't work. So, at last, I gave up.

I woke up, and could still hear those blasting wind chimes.

I tossed and turned in my bed, trying to see if there was anything by the window.

But all I could see was the sun, uncharacteristically dull.

There was wind in the trees and it was about to rain.

I rubbed my eyes and got out of bed. It was my phone that was ringing.

But, before I could pick it up, the ringing stopped.

I wondered who could have changed my ringtone.

Possibly Aarush, our neighbour's son.

Aarush is the smartest 6-year-old I have ever come across who loves his games and gadgets with a passion that is hard to believe. Every evening, he sneaks into our house for fifteen to twenty minutes after playing outside, and asks me to let him play games on my phone. Subway Surfer is his favourite.

I have grown so fond of him in the past few weeks that sometimes, I find myself downloading games for him in my free time.

I dragged myself to the far left of the room and unplugged my phone from the charger. The phone lights were flashing urgently. Four missed calls and three messages, all from one person—Aayesha. All frantic, she told me that Priyanka's grandmother passed away in the morning. We decided to visit Priyanka and meet outside her house at 1 p.m.

I showered, grabbed some coffee, and took off. By the time we were halfway there, it had started pouring really hard. The wipers were working at their highest speed and I could hear the raindrops hammering away at the roof. The roads were blocked, some stretches jammed solid with the sheer number of cars, and I became unsure if I'd be able to make it in time.

'How much time will it take?' I asked the driver.

'At least twenty more minutes, ma'am,' he replied.

I took my phone out of my bag; it was 12.55 p.m.

I called Aayesha to let her know about my situation but she disconnected in one ring.

I thought of sending her a message when my phone beeped with a text from Aayesha asking me where I was. I quickly typed my reply telling her I was running late.

And since there wasn't much to do, I logged on to Facebook. I touched the newsfeed icon, and there it was, Priyanka's status update:

'RIP Granny'

9.46 a.m.

I reached almost in time, I think.

At Priyanka's place, I made sure to fold my hands and bow in respect, and even though I had never met Priyanka's grandmother, my heart sank as I saw them taking her away.

I looked around, hoping to see my friend, but the house was so crowded; she was nowhere to be seen. I was trying to find her so I could console her for her loss, when I heard some of the women there talking about the death.

'It happened this morning, around 9.30.'

I wiped away my tears, turned around, and walked away.

I don't know how people do it. There has been a death in the family. Someone you love has passed away no more than fifteen minutes ago and the first thing that comes to your mind is a Facebook update? I will grow to be a hundred and still not understand this.

Chapter Five

USER-FRIENDLY

This morning, I had a long phone conversation with an old friend.

She was in a new city, where the weather was difficult. Even more difficult was to navigate the traffic of that city. It was a mess, and more than once, she had almost been hurt. Nonetheless, she was keeping it together. Coping. Coping with the disapproval of her parents towards the choices she'd made. Like the choice of leaving the comforts of her parents' home to be on her own in this big, demanding city, trying to make her place in the real world.

She was happy to finally have made friends. Friends who saw her for who she was and not just for her last name. Being part of a group like that was something she had always wanted. She felt happier because she was convinced that she could prove to the whole world that she truly had it in her, that she could succeed at whatever she chose.

So, when the day came, she, like the others, was excited. Excited for the finals. After all the hard work, it was finally the time when it was going to pay off.

For the finals, the students had all been allotted assignments in groups. The assignment hadn't really required an out-of-the-city tour, yet she had taken the opportunity and offered to host her entire study group to travel to her home town. Her family, she insisted, could help; they were in the textiles business, which was also the subject she was studying. And, she told herself, it would also be a wonderful opportunity to introduce to her parents all the people she had been spending so much time with—her friends. Her new friends!

Considering that her hometown was only three hours away by road—and everyone knew of her family's strong background in textiles—everyone readily agreed to the trip. Plus, there was a long weekend in the offing and that had only made things easier.

So, with everyone's parents informed of the travel plans, the group began the journey the next morning.

Being the good hostess she always had been, she invited them home to meet her family. A three-course meal and a tour of the house later, they decided to go visit her grandfather's factory.

The visit was a success—professional, yet warm.

She couldn't stop smiling.

Finally, both her worlds had started to become one.

As the submission deadline grew closer, the group pulled an all-nighter in the living room of her house, taking turns to type. They all felt both content and confident. As they printed the last sheets of paper needed for their presentation on her dad's old printer, she felt a wave of exhaustion and her head began to spin. Slightly dazed, she looked around for her spectacles, but they were nowhere to be found.

'I think I'm going to go lie down for a bit,' she said to no one in particular. Then, she very carefully made it to the bed in her room.

Several hours and endless dreams later, she woke up.

The darkness shocked her.

At first, she couldn't tell if it was the room, or if it was really dark outside. She felt alone, and from the silence, it seemed there was no one around.

She rubbed her eyes and turned to the clock.

It was 6.25 p.m. She had slept for twelve hours straight.

Panicked, she put on her spectacles and searched for her phone. Her heart was hammering; she expected to see at least a hundred missed calls. But to her shock, there was only one.

It was from her mum.

She called her back, 'Hey mom. Where are you?'

'Hi! Listen Prachi, I'm so sorry. I have been at work since morning. The maid told me you were sleeping, so I didn't call you again. Are you feeling all right?'

'Mm... I guess so. I was just too tired, Ma, so I must have dozed off.'

'Yes, you probably needed that. Okay,' she said, 'listen, I'm going to be home as soon as this shipment leaves. Don't have dinner without me.'

'Okay Mom!'

'Acha listen, I thought you said you were supposed to go back with your friends? Didn't you have your submission or something?'

Suddenly, it struck her.

'Mom, I'm going to have to call you back.'

'All right, sweets.'

She tried calling them. Not once. Not twice. At least a dozen times. There was no reply.

After a quiet dinner, she came back to her room. Tossing and turning, that night, she kept replaying it over in her mind. She even worried that she wouldn't wake up in time for the first bus that could take her back to college.

She was surprised that she had slept through her friends leaving. They must have tried to wake her...right? It was an important assignment and the submission wouldn't have been complete without a proper presentation. It was absolutely necessary for all the members of the study group to be present.

She knew it. They knew it.

She took the first bus out, hoping she would reach almost in time.

But, she didn't.

It was over.

The class was empty.

She ran down to the staff room, hoping to see the teacher.

The teacher was there, looking confused.

'I thought they said you weren't coming,' was all she would say.

Chapter Six

HUMANS—THE TAINTED SPECIES

A few thoughts about humans:

Glue is not the only thing that binds things together.

It's also the other things.

The little things.

Bring home a pet, you get attached.

Sit regularly in a particular spot at Starbucks, and you begin to feel that it's yours alone.

Use the same coffee mug everyday, and you find yourself enjoying your coffee more.

Use the same phone or laptop for months, and you can type without looking at the keyboard.

Meet someone often, or talk to her everyday—and you feel you have become inseparable.

But, what happens when it ends?

When your pet dies?

When you reach the cafe to find someone else sitting in your spot?

When your phone falls and breaks, and all your pictures, your memories are gone, just like that?

When the most-called number is no longer a contact in your phonebook?

It is said that every living being that crosses paths with you has something to do with you, and once they have played their role in your life, they leave.

Then, why do we get attached?

Why does it hurt?

Why do we let our guards down?

If their entry and exit is destined, then why can't we prepare ourselves from the very beginning?

We can't because we are humans.

So, what do we do?

We pretend.

We smile.

We bury the pain so deep inside that there is no way it would dare to resurface.

Some people believe in the concept of rebirth, others say we get this chance only once.

We don't know the truth.

But, are we willing to make the best of it?

How often have you told someone you love, that you love them?

A mother doesn't have to tell her children that she loves them; the whole world knows it, but yet she says it, every chance she gets.

Why do you think that is?

Some things are understood, but they have to be said, just because...

They are important.

If there is a problem in a relationship, seldom do people make the effort to make the problem go away.

They prefer talking about each other rather than talking to each other.

What if, we don't get a second chance?

What if, we don't wake up one day?

Only last week, I was watching the news where they were showing how an entire family died while watching television at home, not because of a short circuit or earthquake or food poisoning, but because their house was on the top floor of a high-rise building and an airplane had literally crashed into their house.

A family, watching TV together, under one roof, was finished.

For a moment, just think about the hundreds of unfinished things they left behind.

Perhaps the husband had planned a surprise vacation

for the following weekend, or maybe the wife had planned on cooking the family's favourite dish the next day.

We plan and plan and plan for tomorrow, without realizing there might not be a tomorrow.

We hardly speak our minds or our hearts.

Sometimes, it's our busy lives, at other times, our ego.

And a hundred other things that keep us from feeling what we actually want to feel.

The question is, why?

When you give birth to a child, you want the best for them.

The best care, the best baby products, the best diapers, the best car seat, the best nanny, the best education and the best upbringing.

But, a lot of questions come up too.

Do we let our children be the way they want to be?

Do we let them feel what they want to feel?

We don't.

We constantly try to change them.

There is a difference in changing and moulding.

It starts with making them hold the pencil in their right hand and goes on to deciding what or who they become in life.

We teach our children how important it is to respect our feelings, but when it comes to respecting theirs, we tell them to get over their emotions, their idealism and be a little more practical.

What is this? Parenting?

Or is it hypocrisy in the name of parenting?

Who are we to decide what's good for them when we ourselves don't know what's in store for us tomorrow?

Humans, I tell you!

~

How much is that doggie in the window?
The one with the waggly tail,
How much is that doggie in the window?
I do hope that doggie's for sale.
I don't want a bunny or a kitty,
I don't want a parrot that talks,
I don't want a bowl of little fishies,
*You can't take a goldfish for a walk!**

Read it once, and it sounds like any other nursery rhyme.

Read it twice, and you will feel like reading it again.

The third time round, you will end up singing it out loud.

**Song by Patti Page*

That night, Krisha sang the rhyme, not once, but at least a dozen times; when finally, she had put her two-year-old niece to sleep, she stopped.

Stopped to think about the words of the song she had been singing.

It sounded like such a simple life:

How much is that doggie in the window?
The one with a waggly tail,
How much is that doggie in the window?

She wished there was a place where one could go and buy the people they wanted in their lives. At least then, money would bring in happiness that wouldn't be so temporary. She looked down at her niece, blissfully sleeping on her lap, and then took out her phone and stared at a picture of the man she loved.

I don't want a bunny or a kitty,
I don't want a parrot that talks.

She didn't want to marry someone just because they were financially sound. She didn't want to be with someone just because they followed the same religion as she did.

I don't want a bowl of little fishies.

She didn't want to be with someone just because they were good to look at.

You can't take a goldfish for a walk!

For good looks don't last forever.

She felt that she wouldn't ever be able to love anyone the way she loved him.

She wished she could tell her parents that even though her head knew it wasn't possible, her heart wanted it to happen.

She wanted him so much that she wouldn't let go of the tiny little ray of hope that was left.

I do hope that doggie's for sale.

Chapter Seven

MATTERS OF FACT

I was on the Metro today when I heard some women talking.

'Did you hear about the bomb blast that happened at Connaught Place last night?'

'As a matter of fact, I did.'

'Yeah, I heard. But, you know what?'

'What?'

'The good thing is that this time, it happened after a very long time.'

Ironically, I was on the Metro because I was going to meet my friend, who was a victim of the same blast.

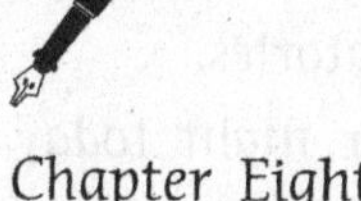

Chapter Eight

FLIGHT MODE

This is an incident that happened on a flight to Delhi.

'Ladies and gentlemen, the captain has turned on the "Fasten Seat Belt" sign.

If you haven't already done so, please stow your carry-on luggage underneath the seat in front of you or in an overhead bin. Make sure your seat back and folding trays are in their full upright position.

If you are seated next to an emergency exit, please read carefully the special instructions card located by your seat. In the event of decompression, an oxygen mask will automatically fall from the cabinet above you. To start the flow of oxygen, pull the mask towards you. Place it firmly over your nose and mouth, secure the elastic band behind your head, and breathe normally.

At this time, we request that all mobile phones and

other electronic devices be turned off. We will notify you when it is safe to use such devices. We remind you that this is a non-smoking flight. Smoking is prohibited on the entire aircraft, including the lavatories.

If you have any questions about our flight today, please don't hesitate to ask one of our flight attendants.

Thank you.'

In the second row, two women were seated next to each other in the pair of seats next to the window. One was obviously younger than the other, but judging just by their clothes, they were from similar backgrounds. Just then, the younger woman turned to the elder, and tapped her on the shoulder.

'Did you hear any of that Mrs... Mrs Mira?'

The young woman had read Mira's name off her boarding pass, which lay on the armrest between them. 'Well, even if you didn't, I'll help you out, I travel back and forth almost every week, you know.'

Mira's forehead wrinkled, and even though she didn't want to, she had to open her eyes. An angry retort leapt to her mind, and she turned, ready to deal with this stranger who had interrupted her rest. Did she have any idea how tired she was and how much she wanted to sleep?

'I did, actually, thanks!' Mira replied sharply to the beautiful girl sitting on her right. The girl, probably in her early twenties, wore a look of helpful sincerity, and despite Mira's tone, still seemed eager to help.

'I'm just really tired,' continued Mira slowly. 'Don't want to open my eyes till we've properly taken off.'

'Rough night?' sympathized the girl.

'Huh! Night? I'd call it a rough week. Stressful.'

'Aww...you do look so tired, Aunty. Is it okay if I call you that?'

'Oh...yes, of course.'

'I thought you were just nervous about the flight.'

'Oh no, flights are fine... I just want to go home.'

'You came to Dubai for some work?'

'Work? No, not really.'

'I came here for a family friend's wedding.'

'Oh okay, hence the jewellery.'

'Yes, jewellery, fully-embroidered clothes, heavy make-up, hair sprays, late nights...phew!'

'Me too. It was really exhausting. Anyway, I feel weddings, these days, are more of a pain than enjoyment.'

'So true, Aunty, so true.'

'I'm sorry. I didn't get your name...'

'Oh, silly me...sorry. I'm Vernica.'

'Vernica. That's a nice name. What do you do, Vernica?'

She paused.

'I'm a healer. Have you heard of Reiki?'

'Hmm... I've heard the word, but never really understood what it was.'

'Okay, let me explain. Reiki is actually a Japanese word, which means cosmic healing energy. It is an ancient form of healing. It is a very simple, yet powerful technique that can be learned and practised by anyone. It's beautiful, Aunty. I mean I feel it's a gift of God and it is known for its phenomenal results.'

'But, how is it done?'

'Let me show you...'

She put both her hands forward, looked Mira in the eye and said, 'Give me your hands.'

Mira looked at her, feeling like a spell had been cast upon her, and put out her hands for the girl to take in her own.

'Okay...now close your eyes and breathe...take long deep breaths.'

Since their seats were among the first ones on the plane, an air hostess showed up as soon as the seat belt sign was turned off.

'Excuse me, Ma'am.'

'Shhh! Not now,' said Vernica, sending the woman away. She held Mira's hands gently at first, as if to gain her trust.

They felt warm.

Next, she started rubbing her hands against Mira's and repeated, 'Inhale...exhale...inhale...' until Mira fell asleep.

'Ma'am! Ma'am!'

When there was no response, the air hostess tried again.

'Madam!'

'Mrs Mira...wake up!'

'Wake up, ma'am!'

'We have to disembark...'

'Huh! What? What did you just say?' demanded Mira, struggling awake.

'Ma'am, we need to leave the plane. We have landed in Delhi and you are the last passenger on board. We need you to come with us.'

'What? When?' Mira felt disoriented.

'It's been a while. We tried waking you up earlier, but you just didn't,' the air hostess shrugged.

'Since the flight was full, we waited for the other passengers to leave and now you are the only one left.'

She handed her a small plastic bottle, 'Here, have some water.'

Mira rubbed her eyes and looked at the air hostess, trying to understand what had just happened. She took the bottle of water, opened the seal and brought it up to her lips.

'But, we just took off, didn't we?'

'No, ma'am. It was a three-hour flight. And you slept through most of it, so if you could please just come with us. You will find your baggage on Belt Number 5.'

Mira was blank; she did not understand how she could have slept through the flight because the last thing she recalled was her conversation with the young girl sitting next to her.

Shrugging, she took a sip of the water, looked around to gather her belongings, and stood up.

'Can I at least use the lavatory?' she asked.

The air hostess looked at her with a frown and said, 'Okay, ma'am, but please make it quick, we need to disembark and we need to do it now.'

Mira took her bag and walked to the toilet. Hanging her bag on a hook, she put her hands under the tap, splashing water on her face.

It was then that she noticed that her fingers were bare.

Her rings were gone, all four of them.

Chapter Nine

APPOINTMENT NO. 2

Two weeks had passed.

At 4.30 in the afternoon, a luxurious car pulled up to the gated driveway of Holy Grace Hospital, and the driver honked the car's horn at the guards to open the gate.

'Madam has an appointment,' he said to the guard who came to the window. Soon, the car was moving inside. A moment later, it arrived at the porch and reached the main entrance of the hospital. Savannah Khanna stepped out, slammed the door shut, and marched into the hospital with a bravado she did not feel.

It had seemed such a good idea at the time and if only Dr Berry had fallen for it, Savannah would have gotten the help she needed without anyone ever having to know that it was her own diary that she was revealing to a perfect stranger.

No matter how warm or comforting Dr Rama Berry had

been, she was ... well, a stranger.

It was an unpleasant feeling to think that she had given the doctor access to the most private of her thoughts—that too for a fortnight!

As Savannah walked uncertainly to the lift and jabbed at the button for the fifth floor, she once again reprimanded herself for being vulnerable. Maybe, I shouldn't have given her my diary, she thought as the lift whirred upward, but I can tell her today I don't need or want her help. I'm just going to take my diary back.

Deep down, however, Savannah knew that it had been her own decision to get in touch with Dr Berry—from the first email to the twenty-fifth. Even so, the prospect of listening to the psychiatrist analyse her own thoughts back to her was more than a little unnerving.

Soon, Savannah entered the antechamber, and was ushered—by a smiling and welcoming assistant, this time—into Dr Rama Berry's private office.

'Doctor,' began Savannah as soon as she crossed the threshold, 'I'm sorry, but there's been a mistake.' She waited for Dr Berry's assistant to leave and close the door before continuing. 'I've come to ask for my diary back.'

'I see,' said Dr Berry gravely.

Her sari today was dark green, the colour of a leaf from the deep forest. 'May I ask why?'

'No, it's ... it's just ...' Savannah shook her head as she took a seat on the sofa once more. 'I want my diary back, that's all. I think I made a mistake by coming here—I'm sorry to have wasted your time, of course, and I will happily…'

'There is no need for worry, my dear,' Dr Berry smiled in response. 'Your diary is, of course, your own. Here,' the elderly psychiatrist unlocked a drawer in her desk with a key from her pocket, and took the blue notebook out. Her sari rustled as she walked over to the sofa, and placed the diary on the table in front of Savannah. She sat down with a calm smile still on her face.

'You do look somewhat better, my dear, I will give you that.' There was only approval in Rama Berry's voice as she ran a doctor's eye over Savannah. 'You still look tired, and you could certainly eat more, but you do look in much better spirits than the last time we met. And before you ask,' the smile turned motherly, 'your secrets are, on my oath as a doctor, safe with me. I wish you only well.'

Savannah smiled despite herself, her reservations beginning to drain away. She picked up the diary, and was just about to put it away, when a sudden frown wrinkled her forehead. 'Wait. What secrets? Did you find something wrong in my diary? Am I…' she took a deep breath and shook her head, but the frown remained fixed on her face. 'Tell me, doctor!'

'My dear,' smiled the elderly woman. 'Please call me Rama. "Doctor" is far too formal. And to ease your concerns, no, I did not find anything "wrong" in your diary. My harshest critique would include that you are, perhaps, overfond of broken sentences, but as they say, it takes all kinds to make the world go round. By "secrets", I meant I understand that what you have shared with me is private, and, unless you yourself permit it, I will not speak of it to anyone. However, it is a pity you do not share your writing with more people. Some of it was really quite good.'

'I ... thank you, Doc-Rama.'

For the first time in weeks, Savannah could feel the beginning of a smile on her lips, an unforced genuine smile of pleasure. Ever since she'd left this office two weeks ago, Savannah had nursed a gnawing sense of worry that the psychiatrist would find her somehow lacking after reading her diary.

'So ...' she ventured.

'So?' asked the psychiatrist, rising to her feet and straightening her sari. 'Oh, yes. You are a talented writer, my child. You should hone your craft. One never knows when or how a well-practised skill may prove useful.'

'That's it?' demanded Savannah, a sudden irritation replacing the relief. 'Two weeks of waiting, and only a "you're a good writer, keep it up"?'

'What did you expect, my dear?' chuckled Dr Berry. 'And did you not yourself say that you felt it was a mistake to come here? I would not force my services upon someone who does not wish them.'

Savannah was quiet for a long moment, her slim fingers subconsciously wrenching at and twisting the diary.

'You really liked it?' she asked finally, with more than a trace of suspicion. 'Which parts?'

'I did not read it to the end, my dear,' replied the psychiatrist, pausing to sit down once more. 'Only some of the beginning, but it was enough for me to appreciate a few of your qualities. You have a sensitive mind and I congratulate you for your depth of vision. Few people see life so clearly.'

'Congratulate me?' demanded Savannah, suddenly angry. 'It's horrible! Everything is so…' her mouth snapped closed, and her lips grew white with the force of her emotion.

'Yes,' nodded the old doctor, and for a moment, her eyes were filled with compassion. 'It can be very…tiring to live your life in such detail.'

Both women were silent for a long moment. Outside, a bird chirruped from somewhere on the tree that loomed over the garden; its call was quickly answered by a dozen more.

'What did you not like of what you read?' asked Savannah suddenly. She was pleased to note Dr Berry's sudden start of attention; then, as though seeing her for the first time, the psychiatrist nodded in appreciation. 'That is a brave approach, my dear,' she said. 'But are you sure you wish to discuss this? I fear I may have been harsh when we met last.

I could have been kinder when asking you who you really were. I would not blame you if you were to choose not to discuss any of this with me.'

'No, I… I want to know.'

Savannah's smile, thought Dr Berry, was just as she had described it on her last visit. The young woman had a generous mouth, more suited to laughing than pouting, and now it was curved in a hesitant smile that nonetheless lit up her face.

'Well,' Rama Berry nodded to herself. 'First, I would tell you that there is nothing wrong with you. I will, of course, ask you to fill out several forms later, and will make a proper diagnosis, but for the moment, I will say that I find nothing immediately unhealthy about your thoughts. To be blunt, however,' Savannah steeled herself as the doctor continued firmly, 'your writing could be less bleak. As I said, I read only a few entries, but even so, I noted that none of them had a positive ending.'

'That's because life is unpleasant,' replied Savannah, her eyebrows arching in surprise. Had the doctor not been able to see something so obvious? The world was a terrible place; there was no getting away from it.

'Since childhood whenever I am unhappy, I write. It helps me release unnecessary stress. If the writing is good enough, I keep it, if not, I tear it out. But, the entire process makes me feel better and I can go back to being myself. That's how

I have taken care of stuff. But, with the passing of time, I have realized, there is so much more to write. Sometimes, things happen to us, other times, to the people we know. But, nobody is paying attention. I want people to realize how they behave. I wish people could be a little more sensitive. I'm writing about the world as I see it.'

'I see,' nodded the doctor, leaning back in her seat. She really is tiny, thought Savannah. Her feet don't even touch the floor when she leans back like that. She suppressed a smile, feeling a sudden flash of hope. Even if the doctor clearly didn't get it, it was good to have someone to talk to.

'Why?' asked Savannah curiously. 'Don't you agree?'

'My view is not the point, my dear,' smiled Dr Berry. Her gaze was abstracted once more, as though considering several things at the same time. 'However, to answer your question, no, I am not quite so... fatalistic myself. While we breathe, there is still time to try and build whatever it is that we consider beautiful; this is how I see it. But, to return to you, my dear, surely there must be something positive?'

'Positive?' Savannah shook her head, her eyes flashing with barely-buried anger. 'No! This world is filled with people, and people are selfish and nasty. Here, I'll show you.'

Chapter Ten

BEWARE OF DOGS

One of my closest friend Amrita, called me last week.

Our friendship reminds me of the hot and cold game we played as kids. When we are in touch, we meet every now and then, share everything with each other, but whenever either of us is busy, we completely lose contact. There have been phases in our lives when we haven't spoken to each other for months.

But, that's the thing about having good friends: one doesn't need to be in touch all the time. Amrita is six years older to me. She is mature and knows what she wants in life. Our friendship is unique in the sense that we can talk to each other about things that we cannot imagine telling anyone else. The rapport is such that no matter how much time has passed, we always start where we left off.

'Can you come over?' were her first words.

At once, I knew something had happened. Something big. I immediately stopped what I was doing and left for her place. Amrita lives across the street from my home so I reached in no time. It was routine to give her a call before entering her house because of the huge signboard that read 'BEWARE OF DOGS'. Her parents find it silly, but she knows how scared I am of dogs/any kind of pet/animal. Sensing from her tone earlier, I didn't feel it was okay to call her, so I asked the guard sitting outside to escort me in. Thankfully her dog, 'Oreo', was at the other end of the garage, sleeping. I quickly made my way in and up, straight to her room. I knocked, but there was no response. I called her name, yet no response. I tried to push the door open and succeeded.

As I entered, I looked around, but I couldn't see her anywhere. I walked towards the toilet since the door was half open and to my surprise, she was sitting on a pouf outside her shower cubicle.

Her face swollen, her eyes cried out. I had never seen her like that.

'What happened?' I rushed towards her. She didn't respond.

'Say something, please.' I held her hands and gave a strong nudge.

She looked into my eyes and said, 'I had a miscarriage!'

'What?' my voice got louder than usual, 'You were pregnant?'

I couldn't believe what I had heard. For the first time, it felt like a lifetime had passed and I had no idea what my friend had gone through. We all knew she was in a relationship with her high-school sweetheart, Harsh and marriage was just a ritual to tick off the checklist. Their relationship was straight out of a fairytale and they were fortunate enough to have their parents' blessings from both sides.

'Where is Harsh?'

What I heard next was unbearably painful even for me, an outsider, who was not directly affected. I could not even begin to feel or understand the level of pain that Amrita must have been going through.

A few weeks ago, she found out she was pregnant. Had it been me or any other girl in her place, we would have freaked out, fainted or even thought of jumping of a cliff because we know how much being pregnant without being married is a taboo in our society. But, this was Amrita.

She was scared yet happy about the whole thing. Her parents were unaware of the change in circumstances; they were, in any case, meeting astrologers to finalize a date for her wedding with Harsh. When she found out, she wanted to run to him and tell him. But, he had been out of the country for work since the last few weeks and wasn't going to return until the next week.

A part of her was upset about having the sequence of events in the wrong order. However, she knew she was going to be his wife soon and that calmed her down. She didn't want to give him the big news over the phone so she decided to restrict the fluttering of butterflies in her stomach until he came back. A few days later, the families met at the astrologer's house. A date was picked in the month to follow. The celebrations began when Harsh's father came up to her and said; 'Why don't you call him and give him the "big news"?'

She knew he was referring to the wedding date and not the news in her head, but she couldn't wait any longer. She ran to the bathroom and, thanking technology in its latest form, she decided to FaceTime him. Eight heartbeats later, her call was answered.

It was Harsh, of course, but only in the background, asleep in his bed. Squinting at Amrita, next to Harsh, was a female, half-groggy, half-awake and half-naked, trying hard to adjust to the sunlight or the light in the room or maybe to the one coming from the phone.

It did not feel like minutes and hours, but only a few seasons that had passed before Amrita could gather herself to stand up and come out. Her pale pink sari was covered in blood.

'I need a change of clothes, Ma,' she told her mom and collapsed.

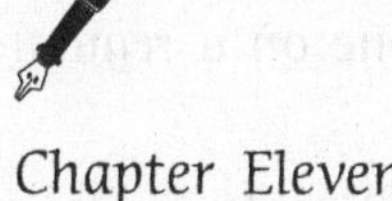

Chapter Eleven

FAMILY TIES

'A son is a son 'til he gets a wife,
but a daughter is a daughter all her life.'
—Emily Giffin

There is a reason this saying is old. It doesn't fit right in today's world.

Naomi and I have been friends for more than a decade now. Be it bunking lectures in the first year of college or studying for the final year exams, we have been together, always.

But, over the years, even though we try to keep in touch, not seeing her often makes me feel that we have become distant. After all, we live in different cities now.

She is busy with her work, her baby, her life, and I have been busy with mine.

Thanks to WhatsApp, we still click pictures of new clothes and ask each other for suggestions before buying, but how much can you talk over messages?

It is different when you meet someone on a regular basis.

You know what they are thinking. You know how they feel.

The use of emoticons is not required to portray the tone of your text.

This afternoon, like many other days, the conversation started with a pair of sunglasses. She liked a pair and sent me a picture to ask for my opinion.

I liked them too.

I wanted to tell her I had liked them for myself and was going to buy them. But, I got tired of typing and I thought of calling her instead.

She was on her way to work.

We were talking, catching up on each other's lives, and then, in a nonchalant manner, she told me that her father was in surgery that very minute. Yes, he was being wheeled into surgery as we were speaking.

I was shocked. Naomi's dad was a pillar of strength for her family. He was healthy, always eating the right kind of food and always making sure to exercise. He didn't even have a chronic ailment, as far as I knew. At some point, we had been such good friends, Naomi and I, that it felt like we were almost living together. So, had I known that he was unwell, I would have gone to see him because even though Naomi herself had moved cities after she got married, I was still living in the same city as her parents.

'Your father is getting operated right now? How come you aren't here?' I asked incredulously. What came next were words that I had never expected would come from a person whom I considered my best friend.

'Actually, my brother is going through a rough patch,' she said.

'Rough patch?' I asked, confused. 'Rough patch as in?'

'As in he is not mentally fit.'

'Not mentally fit?'

'Yeah, over the past few days, he has been having anger issues. He throws things around, screams at everyone and gets angry about anything and everything. Which is why my parents feel I shouldn't come and be disturbed by his behaviour.'

Listening to her talk, my heart sank.

Parents shouldn't have to ask their children to come to their rescue.

They never would; they wouldn't want us to take any trouble. But, does that mean we should give up on them?

On one hand, there was her father who was in surgery; on the other, was her brother with his anger issues. So, her mother was managing everything by herself, because the daughter felt it was okay not to show up and was instead shopping for sunglasses.

When did we become so devoid of feelings?

When did we become people we used to hate?

Do we even like who we have become?

Chapter Twelve

THE WEALTHY WISE

With great power there must also come great responsibility!
—Stan Lee

If only people could understand that, life would have been easier.

Coming from money has its perks, but you can't buy respect now, can you?

Some people think they can, and so they never miss out on a single opportunity to insult the ones they think are below their level of wealth.

Viren was working hard; in fact, very hard. He couldn't tell night from day when it came to work. He had forgotten what Holi/Diwali was. He knew what he wanted in life, and he was moving towards it faster than anyone had anticipated.

He was working so hard that sometimes, I felt he just needed to pause...pause to breathe.

There was an event that our company had to manage, a wedding in Dubai. Not just any wedding. A big fat Indian destination wedding. And Viren was working exceptionally hard, because the woman he was in love with—Rhea—lived there.

Being a workaholic that he was, he had a good opportunity to spend time with her after a long time. Plus, he didn't have to apply for leave to see her; they could meet while he was still working.

I had met Rhea before. She was a simple girl from a demanding social circle, and being in a city like Dubai wasn't very easy for her simple lifestyle. All the more reason for Viren to give her some company and help her navigate her hectic social life.

The wedding was a big hit.

Our company made a huge profit.

The boss was happy so when I suggested we should organize a small party for the employees on our last night there, he agreed readily.

We were a team of about twenty, so I booked a private area at this really fancy bar and I went ahead and called Rhea too.

Viren looked happy.

It was Rhea's birthday the following week and even though it made him a little sad that he wouldn't be with her, he was glad he could see her for some more time, at least. He had asked me to help him pick a present as well.

I remembered her mentioning a bag she had been saving for. And so, when I told about it to Viren, he was more than happy to buy it for her.

Everyone came to the party, including our boss.

He was congratulating all of us for our huge success, when he noticed Viren and his plus one, standing in the corner.

Walking up to them, he said conversationally, 'Meena bazaar, it's a nice place to shop now, isn't it? They sell such good copies, not everyone can tell them apart, so anyone can get them.'

Chapter Thirteen

TIME FOR FIRSTS

Rain, Rain
Go away.
Come again another day,
Ben, my dog wants to play;
Rain, Rain
Go away.

It was 2 p.m., the last time she checked her watch. Another hour had passed and all she could think of was this nursery rhyme she usually sang for her son before putting him to bed.

'Seriously! I mean I don't even sing the regular Bollywood songs I used to in the shower before. My head is so full of all these kids' sing-a-long rhymes,' she had told me once.

'That's what motherhood does to you, doesn't it?'

It makes you let go of your lunch with the ladies.

Suddenly, eyebrows don't look so much in need of a thread running across them. Hair can go another day without being washed. Late night hookah sessions take a back seat to sleepless nights trying to calm a cranky baby.

Why not?

I mean the things we have been doing can actually wait.

Because, now is the time for the firsts.

Their first cry.

Their first smile.

The first fist-finger handshake.

The first bath.

The first feed.

The first burp.

The first toy.

The first rolling over.

The first time they sit up.

The first tooth.

The first sound.

The first response.

The first nod.

I honestly don't know where to stop.

Being a parent is so much more than just bringing a new life into the world.

It's everything around it.

Everything concerning it.

Everything related to it.

It just changes you as a person.

It changes you as a daughter/a son, a wife/a husband, a sibling...

It changes your perspective.

And, why shouldn't it?

After all, it is a big warm beautiful thing.

Correction.

The Most Beautiful Thing!

But, there are people who are waiting to take this very special happiness away from you, sometimes without even meaning to.

Thirty-eight weeks of nausea, eight ultrasounds, hundreds of tears of joyous moments and twenty-four hours of disturbingly painful labour later, when you finally have your baby in your arms, you don't care about what happened before the umbilical cord was cut. At that moment, you are simply stunned; utterly delirious with happiness because of the tiny person that you made.

And all this while, you had only been dreaming about how your baby would look like. But now, here it is, right in your arms, where it belongs. And in this moment, you don't care if it's a he or a she. It's just yours. And, that is all that matters.

You're so full of emotions and then you hear things like:

'He could have had fairer skin, had you eaten the right kind of food during your pregnancy? Remember, when Rashmi's baby was born last month, he was fairer than your baby.'

'Doesn't have a very pretty nose, might need some work.'

Work?

What work?

Suddenly everyone in the room is a cosmetologist.

The poor thing has been in this world for less than an hour.

And, everyone has something to say.

Why are people so insensitive?

Chapter Fourteen

EACH TO HIS OWN

Dr Berry was quiet for a long moment after Savannah had finished reading out the entries from her diary. The doctor was frowning slightly, and staring deeply into the polished woodwork of the long table in front of her. From beyond the window, the birds were calling again, but Savannah paid no attention to the sound, focussing instead on the small woman sitting next to her.

Her heart was pounding, and though she still felt angry, a small part of her was wondering what the doctor would say next. Would she be as indifferent and dismissive as everyone else? Would she tell her to 'get over it', to get on with her life?

'My dear,' Dr Berry began, a soft smile replacing the previously-abstract look. 'I do agree in some part; people can be quite insensitive sometimes. However…'

'Yes?' asked Savannah, brushing aside a long strand of

hair that had fallen over her eyes. 'However?'

'However,' Rama Berry's tone was faintly apologetic, 'I do wonder if you see your own hand in all of this.'

'My own hand?' asked Savannah incredulously. Is this my fault? How? 'What do you mean?'

'Well… I assume, my dear that you write from what you know? That these diary entries are, in some manner, events that you yourself have experienced or heard of?'

'Yes,' Savannah's voice was tight. 'Is that wrong?'

'No, my dear,' the doctor smiled. 'It is just that…the things you write of—such as the insensitivity of others—are things you appear to understand well. You understand that people, on the whole, do tend to behave insensitively, or even maliciously on occasion. Is this not so?'

'Yes,' Savannah's tone had lost some of its edge. 'I suppose. But, how does that change anything?'

'Then—and I ask your forgiveness if what I say appears insensitive—why waste so much of your time thinking about it? Would it not be simpler to just…'

'Just what doctor?' Savannah asked impatiently.

'To just let it go, my dear.'

Savannah let out a frustrated sigh, a dull expression beginning to replace the open anger in her eyes. She's just like the rest of them, Savannah thought dejectedly. This was a mistake. I should leave.

But for a moment, the look of gentle concern on the

doctor's face held Savannah still. There was no judgement in the tiny woman's expression, only a note of genuine interest.

'I…' began Savannah. She shook her head.

'I don't know,' she replied a moment later, frowning at Dr Berry. 'Why does it matter? But, I do think about it, and…'

'And?'

'And I do want to stop!' Savannah almost spat the words out loud.

'I mean…' She had lowered her voice as quickly as it had risen, and now an expression of embarrassed anger coloured her cheeks crimson. Her eyes gleamed with unshed tears. 'I… I don't see the point of anything, anymore. The things I hear and see, I get so affected by them, I can't be myself. The more I write about it, the more I try to get to the root of it. Everything is so pointless, so superficial, it's upsetting. If even having a baby is a…' she trailed off.

'Ah, yes,' Dr Berry nodded. 'If I may ask…'

Savannah nodded jerkily, her eyes fixed on Rama Berry's. The small woman took a moment to adjust her sari before continuing. 'Are you married? Do you have a child, my dear?'

'No,' replied Savannah sharply.

'What about nieces or nephews?'

'Yes, most of my cousins are married and have kids.'

'Well, do you want to get married too and have kids of your own?

Savannah looked away. With her glance stuck at the

window, and after a long pause, she replied, 'Maybe!'

'In that case, as and when your kid grows up, what would you tell the kid about this world?'

'I… I don't understand.'

'My own daughters have grown up and flown away,' smiled Dr Berry. 'I have two, Ramita and Ritika, both beautiful as the sun to me. They're settled now, "abroad", as they say… but, before they left, I made sure to teach them as much as I knew about the world, about how to protect themselves, and which experiences I found to be most beautiful. Fifteen or twenty years from now, when your children are old enough—perhaps preparing to leave their own home—what would you tell them?'

'I… I would tell them to trust no one,' replied Savannah fiercely. But, what does all of this have to do with my diary?

'But, you are trusting, my child,' chuckled Dr Berry, a smile breaking on to her face. Savannah smiled uncertainly, surprised by how warm and sincere Dr Berry's amusement seemed to be. 'Why do you say that, doctor?'

'My dear,' Dr Berry's smile grew broader, 'I do not counsel suspicion as a general course of action. Healthy minds should be able to experience and grow, and for that, trust is required. However,' her eyes were twinkling, 'for a woman to be so trusting that a stranger could steal the rings off her very fingers…'

Savannah coloured. 'That didn't happen to me. It

happened to my aunt,' she replied, perhaps a little too quickly. 'That wasn't me. I…'

Dr Berry's chuckle faded, though a gleam of alert amusement remained in her eyes.

'Are you telling me to be more suspicious?' demanded Savannah a moment later, her embarrassment refusing to fade. 'What sort of advice is that?'

Her reply came out sharply, as though Savannah was informing a carpenter that she did not like the quality of their work. There was an instant of charged silence, and then Dr Berry nodded. 'I apologize, my dear,' she replied simply. 'I was not making light of your pain.'

Savannah's nod was stiff, her cheeks red with both anger and shame, and a strong desire to simply stand up and leave was beginning to overwhelm her. I already have my diary back. I don't need to listen to…

'What I wanted to tell you, my dear,' Rama Berry's voice was crisp and professional, 'is that I stand by my initial judgement. There is nothing… wrong with you, medically speaking. You have a healthy—albeit troubled—mind, and again, I must commend you on your sensitivity. It is a gift, in my experience. I, personally, do not see any need for my services, but I will, of course, be happy to schedule a more detailed examination to confirm my diagnosis. Of course,' her tone grew momentarily both amused and weary, 'I must warn you, my dear, there are many, many forms to be filled.'

'But, you said I had a hand in...in the reason I'm here for,' Savannah's voice had a touch of sullenness. Even if she doesn't understand a thing, thought Savannah, she's still my best hope. No one has ever listened to me, to this extent.

'Yes,' nodded Rama Berry. 'You are aware of the ideas that you write about, but you do not review your perception of the world in light of what you know, my dear. You are now more than a young girl; you are a grown woman, and a rather pretty one at that, of about twenty-five summers, if I am not wrong. So, it should no longer surprise you that men can lie and women can steal; or that people can envy each other enough to the point of violence.'

'But, they shouldn't!'

Rama Berry shrugged. 'If we wish for the right to not be questioned and to do as we wish,' she spoke as though quoting, 'then we must fight for others to have those rights too.'

'So, people should be allowed to cheat, and steal, and...'

'It is not a matter of allowing, my dear. It is what people have been observed to do—both in this day and age, and in the past. We all come from different values, backgrounds and beliefs. What is right for you may not be right for your neighbour. Knowing this, would it not be better to protect oneself, and then, hope for the best. Don't you agree?'

'I...yes, I suppose,' replied Savannah, nodding slowly. Her anger, however, was burning bright. It had been stoked by the memories the doctor was prodding at. There had been great deal of laughter, around dinner tables and on cell phones, once the story of the stolen rings had gotten out. She had sworn everyone she had told this story to absolute secrecy, but they had talked to each other anyway. 'So, you are saying I shouldn't... that I just shouldn't care? That people are superficial, that we should accept... accept such a... fake world! That everyone's so selfish! That they're just in it for a laugh, and whatever they can grab along the way! How can I ignore...'

'You should not ignore anything,' replied Rama Berry cautiously.

'One must learn whatever there is to be learned; but at the same time, you must not allow yourself to become so deeply invested in matters outside your control. How other people behave is something for them alone to ponder over.'

She stood, smoothing her sari once more, and for a moment, Savannah was struck by how peaceful the elderly doctor looked. Dr Berry does not seem stupid, she thought, but if she's so much older than me and has even an ounce of sense, why isn't she as angry as I am?

'If you wish, my dear,' Dr Berry's voice was firm, 'I will schedule another appointment for us, two weeks hence. However,' she smiled softly, 'I will have to ask for your diary back. I see that I have some serious reading to do.'

Savannah stood up too, suddenly uncertain. *Just leave,* the angry part of her whispered. There's no point. She won't get it.

An instant later, Savannah thrust the diary at Dr Berry, before turning and walking out of the door.

Chapter Fifteen

SUMMER OF 2006

It was an intense summer.

Sometime in May.

Another semester at college had ended, so like every other outstation student, I too decided to go home for the break and spend time with Mom, enrol myself for guitar lessons, or perhaps do something else. Something constructive. I was all packed to leave, and took a cab to the bus station. I paid the cab guy, and found myself a seat in the waiting room. After all it was May.

The next bus home was in half an hour.

I bought a magazine, a big bag of chips and a diet soda from the cafe. I started walking towards the bus, lost in my own thoughts, when suddenly I was interrupted by the sound of a car.

I turned around and saw a white car screeching

to a halt; it came and stopped pretty close to the bus. The door on the right opened, and a guy came out of the driver's seat and banged the door close. Tall, fair, good-looking and in quite a black mood at the time.

He got off in such a rush that he didn't even notice that his wallet had fallen out of the car. He just marched around the car, to the co-driver's seat, and opened the door.

Out came a young girl, probably around the same age as him; but she didn't look angry. She looked unhappy.

Like something bad had just happened.

She got out of the car and started walking towards the bus, her gaze fixed on the road, as if she didn't want to look at anyone.

When she came closer, I realized that she was crying.

They parted ways without even a goodbye—not even looking at each other.

He quickly rushed back to the driver's side of the car, picked up his wallet from the ground, got into the car, and roared away as though he was rushing to put out a fire.

I noticed that the girl didn't have any luggage.

Not knowing what to do, I climbed into the bus and got my seat.

As the crying girl was getting on my bus, the conductor looked at her and said, 'Madam, didn't you just get here this morning?'

She looked at him, despair in her eyes, and replied in a deep soft voice. 'Yes', she said. 'I did...but it wasn't enough.'

She came and sat next to me.

Her gaze fixed on her bare ring finger.

It was then that I realized the purple around her eyes was not make-up.

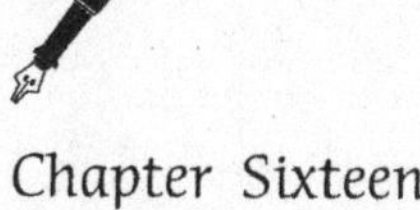

Chapter Sixteen

COURTSHIPS

Met once on Monday.
Twice on Tuesday.
Wore best on Wednesday.
Tried harder on Thursday.
Fought on Friday.
Stooped lower on Saturday.
Stepped out on Sunday.

It was only a few days ago that you had congratulated them. Maybe, you thought, it was finally time to start believing in fairy tales again...when you find out that they have called it off.

Some blame the astrologer.
Some talk of secret affairs.

Some are devastated.
Some end up fully wasted.
Some are glad they didn't tie the knot.
Others try hard to plan and plot.
He says, 'It's her.'
She says, 'All him.'
You have no clue whatsoever, even when you are the next of kin.

Late Night Entry:

I had just got off the phone with Payal. She got engaged last month and started to behave as though she had become 'The First Lady' of our country, giving herself airs to a level that I had neither expected nor could tolerate.

'My engagement has been called off, Savvy,' she said in a weak voice.

'What? When? Why?'

'This morning.'

'What? And you are telling me now? But, why? What happened?'

'Their family astrologer told them that if they... if they brought me into the house, there would be a threat to someone's life.'

'A threat? Are you kidding me? You are the last person who can ever be a threat to anyone!'

'The astrologer has told them that the day I get married in their family, the head of the family will lose their life.'

Saying that, she hung up.

P.S.
How can someone's mere presence be the reason for another person losing their life? How can anyone believe such utter nonsense?

Chapter Seventeen

HEAR, CHANT, PREACH, ABIDE

There is a thing.
A thing about writing.
Some do it for the money.
Some for fame.
Others as a hobby.
With me, it's different.
I do it for the peace and the quiet.

With a pen in my hand, I get to set aside the things and feelings that I may or may not want to think about. I get to meet another side of me. I allow my thoughts to flow and it helps me know myself better. If only I could use this better side of me and apply it to my life, I could even be happy!

We see something on the television that touches

our heart and we promise ourselves to bring a change in our life; but do we?

Someone once asked me, 'What is the point of buying a ticket and keeping it in your pocket when you don't intend on boarding the flight?'

I wasn't sure I quite understood it, then. I do now.

People are so blinded by certain religious beliefs that they don't try to question superstitions. They don't feel the need to see logic. It is hard to understand that people who claim to spend more than a couple of hours everyday meditating in God's name, still believe that giving birth to a male child trumps over bearing a female child.

He wouldn't cross the road no matter how much he wants to, cursing the poor cat for having crossed his path.

She wouldn't mind taking the last slot available for a pedicure, but if she were to see someone cut his or her nails at the same time at home, she would throw a fit.

They hang lemon and chilly totems outside their homes, in their cars, to ward off the evil eye, and when it begins to rot, they replace them with fresh ones.

But, where do the old, rotten ones go?

They are thrown on the streets in a hope that someone else would step on them and take away the negativity off our lives into their own. How convenient!

Since childhood, I have heard people say things like, 'The Great Almighty gives us every breath we take. All the hardships we face are a result of our karma. We smile because God wants us to. Every individual has a journey he has to complete.'

We hear it. We chant it. We preach it, but do we really abide by it?

If this is our journey, aren't we supposed to learn from it?

Or are we supposed to follow our superstition blindly, no matter who it hurts?

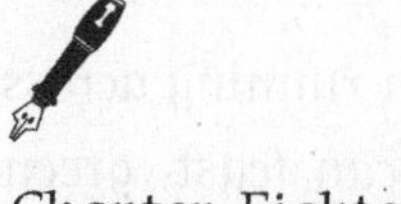

Chapter Eighteen

SHOWER OF BLESSINGS

Being the first-born child, Aarohi was always the first one to experience everything.

The first one to go to school.

The first one to throw tantrums during her early teens.

The first one to finish school, the first one to graduate.

The first one to get married and also, the first one to have conceived.

She was entering unknown territory.

She was nervous and felt like a new person, but she had friends and family to support her. Her friends were not experienced in childbirth, but their presence still helped.

She was about seven months along in her pregnancy

when one day, they took her out saying it was 'just lunch', when it was actually, a surprise baby shower.

The décor was breathtaking.

Beautiful ribbons in yellow and green running across the welcome banner. A delicious Moroccan feast, green iced teas to sip on. The food, the flowers, the balloons, the ambience, everything was just perfect.

There were games. There was cake. There were friends and friends of friends, some taking pictures and others recording videos of these special moments.

It took her a while to take it all in, but when she did, she was sure that had she known about it, there wasn't a single thing she would've wanted to do differently.

She felt elated and so did the baby. She could tell.

It looked like a page from a fairytale, until she heard someone say, 'How do you girls decide to get pregnant so soon, and how do you manage to go all the way?'

Aarohi was confused. She wasn't sure if the girl had actually spoken those words or she had misheard.

'All the way?' she asked.

'All the way, as in, to nine months,' replied the friend of a friend. 'In case I ever plan on having a baby, I would get a C-sec after the seventh month.'

'And why would you do that?' asked Aarohi in a not-so-pleasant tone.

'If you come to think of it, it's a practical way to do it, you know, because the major stretch marks begin to appear only after the seventh month. I'm just saying, one stone, two birds.'

There were at least a dozen replies that Aarohi could think of to shut her up—having a healthy child being the first on her list—but she chose to be quiet.

A few seconds passed by.

She turned around, and looked for a human to speak to.

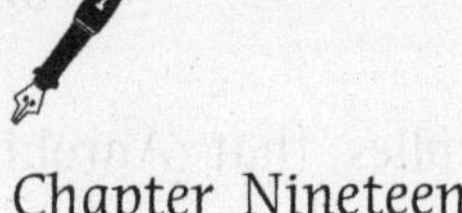

Chapter Nineteen

SHOW ME THE MONEY

These days, if you can't be home for the India–Australia match, you record it. You want to go out on a Saturday night; you record the Filmfare Awards, and watch it on Sunday. You want to switch between sitcoms, record them, and skip the ads.

Back when I was a kid, we used to finish our homework in time to watch TV. Mom would finish off her daily chores. Dad would return from work, and we would all sit down to watch TV together.

No recording, no skipping ads. I think that's the reason, we still remember the advertisements from back then.

There was this one ad in particular that for some reason got stuck in my head:

'There are some things money can't buy.'

I guess we proved them wrong now, didn't we?

I still remember that day at school when every single person—friends, classmates, schoolmates, teachers—turned around for a second glance to make sure it was me they had seen.

I had lost seven kilos in ten days. My uniform didn't fit me the way it used to, I was pale. Dengue had gotten the better of me. I remember not having the energy to even carry my school bag. I asked for help.

The reason I got discharged from the hospital as early as I did was that my Class X board examinations were only a few weeks away.

I was scared. I remember thinking that I would not be able to prepare. All that I had learnt, all that I had memorized seemed to have left my brain. So, I had to start again.

I was in school then, and being stressed about examinations came naturally. We were trained to work under pressure, and so I managed to get a good score. It made my mom proud.

That was then.

Today, when I look around, I feel that all that stress, all the pressure, all those equations, maps, tables, formulae, were a waste. Schools and colleges don't really care about the quality of education anymore. The only numbers they are concerned about these days are the ones that have Gandhi printed next to them.

Today, it is even possible to make someone else take an exam in your name while you are home, doing nothing.

How did we come this far? Where are the values?

Your child is not a fan of books—fine. He is not goal-oriented—agreed. Let them be. They will pick another hobby. Why show them the easy way out?

It's clearly a result of cutting class, especially the one that taught moral science.

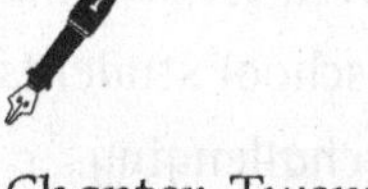

Chapter Twenty

THE PRINCESS

A new story:

The Princess

Dhruv and Mahima were married and in love.

They had moved to Bengaluru only five years ago. And, the city had welcomed them with open arms.

Dhruv, an architect, was so passionate about his work that he often got home late. Mahima, on the other hand, had a 7-to-3 job, teaching at a renowned high school. But, by the time she would reach home, it would be evening.

When she got pregnant, she decided to take it easy.

Not working was not an option, because there was now an extra mouth to feed—a whole new member in the family. They would be struggling to make ends meet; so, she decided to take up a job at a playschool instead.

This had the added advantage that it would give her first-hand experience of handling smaller children. To be perfectly honest, she was somewhat relieved; she would no longer have to deal with spoiled high-school students who were, more often than not, pretty challenging.

Her new place of work was quite unlike the older one. To begin with, it was just a fifteen-minute walk from where she lived. Also, the timings were great, especially important considering she might even at times have to leave her baby at home.

Dhruv was not in favour of her working at first, but when she explained to him that she only needed to go in to work for two hours a day, he stopped to think. It couldn't be all that bad. All they needed to do now was to hire a good nanny.

Seven interviews and lots of paperwork later, they hired Sunita, a middle-aged widow. They had decided to hire her mainly because she had no family of her own; both of them had felt that she would, therefore, be even more dedicated to her work.

Some months later, their baby was born.

'It's a girl!' Dhruv shouted his lungs out, while he cut the umbilical cord with his trembling hands. He looked at the woman he loved and kissed her sweaty forehead, so happy that the little bundle of joy had finally arrived.

They named her Amira—their princess. She was treated like one too.

Their days were filled with tiny yawns and a million smiles. And so, time flew and she was one!

They celebrated with a big bang, and now it was time for Mahima to resume work.

The first day was difficult, but thankfully, Sunita had worked with them long enough to be trusted and left alone with the baby.

Mahima had set Amira's sleeping pattern so that the baby would wake up just half an hour before Mahima got home herself. So, everyday, Mahima would come home right in time for Amira's 'breakfast'.

Mahima was happy how things had worked out. Everything was going perfectly for her.

A loving husband, an adorable daughter, a decent job and a wonderful nanny.

That particular day, Mahima knew she would be late. The school was taking the kids for a picnic to a deer park, not very far from where she lived. At first, Mahima asked for a leave, but the principal refused since it was the school's first picnic, and they wanted as many teachers around as possible, to watch over the children.

It was a huge responsibility, especially with such small children.

Mahima knew she would be an hour late getting home, so she had prepared Amira's breakfast before going to work. Sunita was to give Amira a bath and make sure she ate.

The picnic was a lot of fun.

Everyone was having a good time, when suddenly, it started raining.

The principal instructed the teachers to herd the children back to their respective buses and head back to school.

The bigger the city, the more the traffic...and rain always makes it worse.

Mahima looked at her watch, calculating how long it would be until her daughter woke. In a way she was happy; it had rained early enough that she would be able to get home in time, if only there was no traffic.

However, the city had other plans.

They had been stuck in traffic, sitting immobile on the road for at least twenty-five minutes, and Mahima could feel herself losing patience. It was humid too, especially inside the bus, so she decided to open a window.

She felt better, even though the cacophony of sound coming from the traffic outside was deafening. Horns were blaring, people were arguing in loud voices, hawkers were yelling even louder, and there was more than one cow sitting smugly across critical junctures in the road.

They were at a traffic light, and Mahima could see the amber light glowing balefully from perhaps a hundred metres away.

Amongst the different noises that were coming from outside, she heard a cry—the cry of a baby.

An instant later, she had jumped up from her seat with a cry of her own.

'What is it?' her colleagues asked, surprised by Mahima's sudden movement.

'It's Amira,' replied Mahima as she rushed towards the door of the bus.

'What?', 'Where?' and 'Stop!' were the loudest replies; but, Mahima had already got off the bus.

She could see a lady in a half-torn purple saree carrying a child in her arms and walking around, knocking at the car windows, begging for money.

For a moment, Mahima thought she had made a terrible mistake and she started to regret her actions, kicking herself, mentally, thinking how crazy she must have seemed rushing off the bus like that. It must have been another baby's cry; there was no way it could have been Amira, she thought. The baby that the lady on the street was holding could not possibly have been Amira.

Repeating this, Mahima forced herself to turn around and start walking back to the bus, when she heard the baby's cry again.

She stopped, closed her fists tightly, took a long, deep breath and turned around.

What she saw stopped her world for a second. Everything got blurred, and she knew, somehow, instinctively, that if she didn't fight it, she would faint. She gathered her courage and ran towards the beggar lady in the purple sari.

It was Sunita, her nanny, and she held in her arms Mahima's princess, Amira, wearing nothing but a dirty old rag, torn and soiled and wet. Her nose was runny and her eyes red, from all the crying.

To have found her daughter, stolen from her own crib, in such a terrible state, out on the road, when she should have been at home! Mahima felt as though her heart was going to leap out of her chest. With trembling hands, she snatched her daughter away from the wretched woman—who released the baby quickly, and ran away.

Mahima began to run herself; she did not know where she was going, or why she had to run. In the distance, she could hear her colleagues shouting for her to stop, to slow down. Soon, her lungs were burning, but despite feeling that she had to stop, she kept running until she had come far away from that awful jam.

She found shelter under a tree, heaving and panting, as she tried to catch her breath. Amira, wonder of wonders, was not crying; she was studying her mother's face with a curious, inquisitive gleam in her eyes.

Since it was raining, Mahima took off her dupatta, thinking to shelter her baby. She stopped, and wiped Amira's face clean first. Then, since the rain seemed to be getting stronger, wrapped it snugly around her baby.

She looked around warily and gathered some energy. She wiped away her tears as best she could, and wandered fearfully until she came across an old man on the street who allowed her to borrow his phone.

Mahima called Dhruv who rushed to his family's rescue.

Amira caught a cold and fever and took days to recover. Even though Dhruv wasn't there, and hadn't heard the wails of his crying baby, hadn't seen her in that pitiful state, he was still rattled, and took a few weeks off work to take care of his family. As for Mahima, she still wakes up from the middle of her sleep, shivering.

They left Bangalore soon after and never returned.

Chapter Twenty-One

ONCE UPON A NIGHT

It's pretty quiet for a weekend, that too at such a brand new club.

Even the manager seemed surprised. Earlier today, he had convinced me that it was going to be a super busy night when I called to ask about reservations. He looked a bit of a fool now, but at least he had the grace to look surprised.

Whoever said 'old habits die hard' was right. As usual, I was the first one to reach the venue.

It's easy to yell at old friends for being late, but difficult to separate logic from their excuses.

Over the next hour, they began to arrive; single, in pairs, or in larger groups. Within the next hour, they were all there. We exchanged pleasantries, ordered our drinks and began talking, when a friend's phone buzzed.

She took some time attending to it, and her face went through a variety of expressions.

'All well?' I asked.

'It's disturbing,' she replied, her eyes still locked on her phone.

'What is it?' I was curious.

'Wait, I'll post it on the group,' she said.

We all reached for our phones, and within seconds, we received the video.

It was taken in a secluded corner of some mall.

A kid, who looked closer to three-four years old, was sitting in one of those trolley kind of cars that we see in malls these days. He was with a boy, a domestic help or caretaker, who was probably in his early twenties. The video was taken from behind a pillar and from a distance, so it was not really clear. Nonetheless, it was easy enough to understand what was happening. The caretaker was trying to forcefully kiss the little boy. The poor kid kept pushing him away, but he wouldn't stop. At the end of the video, he managed to kiss the kid on the mouth, leaving the kid feeling helpless.

The video made me feel not only helpless but also angry. Helpless because you know what's going to happen next and yet, you cannot stop it from happening, and angry because, the person behind the pillar took the time to stop what he/she was doing to hide and make a video.

Why didn't they just stop that person from doing what he was doing?

Why didn't someone take responsibility, to save the innocent child from this sick, ugly act of molestation? It's a shame, really.

It was the first time that our weekly night-out ended as quietly as it had begun.

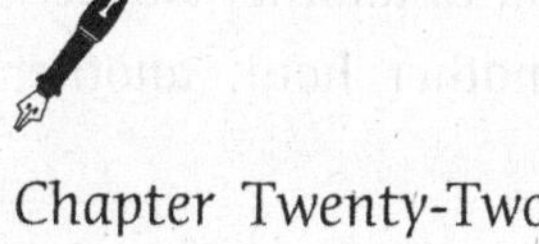

Chapter Twenty-Two

FAKE-ISM

How much can you stretch the same band?
How elastic can your gum be?
How much can you stretch one thing?
I mean how long can you keep talking about the same thing?

Monday, Tuesday, Wednesday,
Noon, 3 p.m., 11.45 p.m.
2010...2011...2050...
Even the movie didn't do well.

Okay, so you have a fleet of cars—great.
You have the best of clothes—agreed.
You have the best jewellery there is—accepted.
So then, what next?

Are we going to start talking about it during drinks and go on till the end of the evening?

Or are we ever going to move on to another subject?

It feels like one more day, another hour, another minute is wasted.

~

Bad Hair Day:

It was a friend's birthday, and I was invited to the party. I went to buy her a present.

It was just one of those days when you don't feel like dressing up. I was in my casuals, and there is a reason 'bad hair day' became a cliché. But, I just decided to hit the mall anyway.

While in search for an appropriate present, I bumped into an old friend.

I had forgotten about the way I was dressed, but I was quickly and terribly brought back to reality. At first, it was just eye contact, but soon her eyes began to roll, and in no time, she looked way.

She did not even think it was important to introduce me to her friends.

Just because I wasn't dressed well?

I was her friend. So what if I wasn't well-dressed?

I was still me.

My light comfortable loafers suddenly felt heavy as I started to walk away.

I mean, what happened to the 'we'll hold hands and skip together' part?

I haven't called her since. Nor do I intend to.

I walked in the dark, with a heart full of love.
I was carrying my soul, when Dior was enough!

Chapter Twenty-Three

THE WET BED

She felt soaked, and even though she had just woken up from deep sleep, she was too embarrassed to open her eyes.

The feeling reminded her of her childhood days.

When she was old enough to be toilet-trained, yet too young to control the effects of her nightmares on her tiny bladder. Every time she had a bad dream, she would wake up soaked in her own urine.

But, she was a kid then, and now, she had a daughter old enough to go to college.

'How could I have wet the bed?' she thought to herself.

Her eyes still closed, she tried really hard to recall but all that she could remember was—voices. They were nothing like the nightmares that troubled her when she was eight. These were different.

Whispers.

Scary whispers.

'How will I face Ram?' she thought to herself.

'What will I tell him?'

'How could I wet the bed?'

It kept eating at her.

Minutes felt like hours, until she gathered enough courage to open her eyes.

It wasn't her that had wet the bed.

It had been him. He was covered in blood.

They had brutally murdered him in his sleep and had taken away everything they had ever possessed.

She felt a deep pain, but didn't know what was hurting. Soon, that thought fled as the pain became unbearable. Her body stiffened in shock, and even though she wanted to, she couldn't move.

Her eyes staring into blankness. Her head full of voices.

They had not been voices from a dream. They had been real. Actual voices from that night.

It had been a nightmare after all.

Chapter Twenty-Four

THE FARMERS' MARKET

The farmers' market in Delhi happens on different days in different areas. They are often named after the days of the week.

For instance, in most areas of South Delhi, there is a Sunday Market. In West Delhi, it is a Thursday Market. Central Delhi has a Monday Market, and so on.

It was a Thursday, and as usual, I was out and about to buy fresh fruits and vegetables.

How lovely it is to look at heaps of colourful ripe fruits, and fresh green vegetables that you don't find at regular supermarkets!

As usual it was crowded.

I often decide what I'm going to cook while waiting for my turn to pay. It feels good to know that it's fresh produce and not something from cold storage.

When I reached the end of the market, I noticed something unusual.

Week in and week out, I had been coming to this farmers' market and not once had I seen this particular booth. I stopped to see what was it that they were selling.

To my surprise, the person sitting in the chair was not a stranger. I knew him. He was a person who worked as a peon at the Blind School across the street.

There have been several occasions when our family has been there to help out in any way we could. I knew him by his first name.

'Arjun uncle, what are you doing here?' I asked.

He knew me too, but he looked away, as though he didn't want to make eye contact. Something didn't feel quite right.

'Answer me,' I said in a rather commanding tone.

The man couldn't look me in the eye.

I looked around the booth and froze. I picked up my grandmother's shawl out of the other familiar clothes I could see hanging off the rack.

'This wasn't for sale!' I yelled, angry at such misuse.

The donation had not reached the blind children.

It was never intended to.

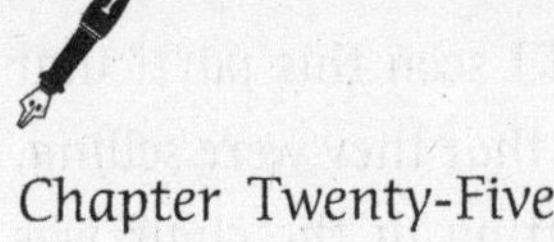

Chapter Twenty-Five

A HELPING HAND

Sixty-nine years old Amarnath Rathore lived with his 14-year-old granddaughter Arandita on the ground floor of his two-storey building in Colaba.

Having lost their family in a car crash, they were the only two left—Arandita and her grandfather—and this old property they lived in. The expenses of a not-so-spoilt teenager were met with the grandfather's only source of income, the rent that he got from the families living on the two floors above him.

On the first floor, lived a newly-wed couple, Rohit and Shivani.

On their first day, they didn't bring much stuff, but on the days that followed, they brought a great deal, most of it noisy. Sometimes it was their new furniture being delivered. Most often, it was their friends arriving or leaving.

Amarnath often woke up in the middle of the night to ask them to keep it down.

It was just last week that they had bought a new car.

The new Mercedes S-Class. A car big enough for five when they were just two, Amarnath had often thought to himself. But, unlike his tenants on the first floor, he was very happy with the two that were staying on the second floor.

Kartik, in his final year of engineering, used to spend the entire day out of the house, only returning late in the evening. The boy would usually come home tired; so exhausted that all he could do was finish his dinner. Quite often, he would doze off even before having his meal. His roommate Raghav, on the other hand, worked the night shift at a call centre. So, the ones that most landlords would assume to be troublemakers were actually the quiet ones, in this case. However, despite the dislike he felt for the newly-weds who had moved in above his roof, Amarnath kept the peace.

He had no choice, really. Amarnath had to somehow come to terms with the arrangement; he needed the money and the newly-weds, the address. After all, Colaba was one of the best areas in Mumbai.

It was a Monday morning and like every other morning, Arandita packed her lunch and left for school, leaving her retired grandfather in the company of his armchair and tea. Having finished his second cup, Amarnath went out to pick up his copy of *The Times of India*, when he saw Kartik standing in his balcony.

'Monday morning blues?' he asked looking up at Kartik.

'Didn't sleep very well uncle...taking the day off,' replied a dull voice.

'Oh! Go get some rest then and once you're up, come and join me, I'll prepare some tea for you too.'

'Maybe I will in a while. Thank you uncle!'

Amarnath was tired from lifting his head up for so long so he gave a thumb's up in Kartik's direction and slowly walked back inside.

A few moments later, when he rose from his armchair to go to the kitchen, he heard an unbearably loud explosion. At first, he thought he was having an attack of some sort, that death had finally arrived; but, when he glanced out of the window and saw the neighbours coming out of their houses and running towards his own, he realized they were all looking at the top of his building.

He rushed out towards his balcony to get a better

look; but, before anyone could react, there was a loud roar of crackling fire, and a whooshing sound. The heat suddenly began to rise, and quickly, much too quickly, the second floor of the building was engulfed in flames.

The old man, who could barely walk without support, ran towards his wall-mounted telephone and called for a fire brigade and then an ambulance. His hands trembling, his legs shaking, he again ran outside, not even bothering to put the earpiece back on its holder as he rushed screaming for help.

A few moments later, the shocked crowd gathered around the burning building watched as Kartik painfully made his way down the spiral staircase on the left. His clothes were covered in his blood, and his face was clearly burned, but somehow, he managed to make his way downstairs.

Even though he was writhing in pain, people waited for the ambulance to arrive.

Amarnath tried to stop a car that was passing by; he didn't want to wait another second. It looked familiar. It approached close to the building as it slowed, and then abruptly sped up.

'Shivani, come back!' shouted Amarnath as loudly as he could. 'Shivani!' he shouted at the top of his voice.

Yet, she drove away. Amarnath could see her parking her car at the next building.

A young boy from next door came by with a bucket of water and splashed it on Kartik as he lay moaning on the ground.

A few seconds later, Shivani appeared, walking in the direction of her house.

'What happened, uncle?' she asked, nervously. 'How did the fire start?'

Amarnath could see that she was avoiding looking at Kartik.

'There has been a blast,' he shouted in reply. 'Where is your car, Shivani? Bring it; we need to take him to the hospital now!'

'What? How? We can't... I mean...'

'Look at his condition! We don't have time to waste! Call Rohit, or you go and bring your car yourself!'

'Rohit is not here, uncle. I just dropped him off at the airport. You need a car? Actually mine is new... Wait, I'll just call for a cab. It will be here in the next five minutes.'

Later that evening, every news channel was showing the story.

'AC blast in Colaba.
Young engineering student succumbs to injuries.
Ambulance didn't reach in time.
Strong winds fanned the fire.

> Cheap-quality furniture, highly combustible in nature, made the fire spread quickly.'

Little did they know that it wasn't only the furniture that was cheap.

Chapter Twenty-Six

THE WORLD WE LIVE IN

A fortnight after her last meeting with Dr Rama Berry, Savannah Khanna's car once more approached the gates of Holy Grace Hospital.

Inside the car, Savannah appeared to be a changed woman. The soft bags that had once been so prominent beneath her eyes had receded to a great degree. And, despite the worried frown that drew her pencil-thin eyebrows together, she appeared far calmer than her last visit. Even so, she had spent the two weeks between meetings in a flurry of emotions, her mood swinging from worry and irritation to hope and then back again. An unintended—but positive—consequence was that she had been unable to sit still for any length of time, even in her own room. She'd taken to walking long brisk rounds of the park outside her house, with her 3-year-old niece whenever her cousin was visiting.

Savannah had returned home each night both tired and worried, but her exhaustion had driven her to eat, and then to a deep slumber. So, after ten days of this, she felt more alive than she had in months. The added anticipation of what Dr Berry would say today had even driven Savannah out of bed at six in the morning. And, though it was now almost six in the evening, she could feel her spirits lifting. At least, now she had someone to talk to.

The trip to the main door of the hospital, through the foyer and then up the elevator was by now a familiar one. Soon, Savannah found herself being ushered into Dr Berry's private office.

'Ah, my dear, welcome,' smiled the doctor, getting up from behind her table. She had been going over some notes, Savannah could see; the broad surface was scattered with papers and books, and a notepad full of scratchy handwriting sat atop it. 'I finished reading your diary only last night. I must congratulate you.'

'I…thank you, doctor,' replied Savannah uncertainly, smiling politely in reply. She took a seat on the couch as she'd done on the two previous visits, and soon Rama Berry was sitting next to her. The blue diary was in her lap, as was the pad with her scratchy notes; and on this day, her sari was of the deepest blue, edged in grey embroidery.

'Your diary fulfilled the promise of its beginning, my dear,' continued Rama Berry once she was comfortably seated. 'Your writing style, my dear—and I say this objectively, as someone who has read a great deal of other people's writing—is both effortlessly easy to read and capable of being tremendously poignant. I quite enjoyed some of the entries, especially the one about the ... what was it called ...' She broke off, rustling through her notes for a moment. 'Ah yes,' she smiled. 'The Wet Bed. I quite enjoyed the twist at the end.'

'You liked that one?' asked Savannah, half-scandalized. Dr Rama Berry had begun to remind Savannah of her own grandmother, who had been a sweet, gentle lady who only lost her temper when embarrassed ... which reading that particular story certainly would have made her.

'Yes,' smiled Dr Berry. 'Very much. It was so vivid! And, the embarrassment is described so accurately! And, it is so true about life as well. I often find that people lie awake, pretending to be asleep, because of a problem that doesn't even exist.'

'But ...' interrupted Savannah, the frown back on her face, 'in the story, she woke up to see her husband dead!'

'Better than lying awake all night wondering if she had wet the bed!' said Dr Berry with a shrug. 'Even if the truth is horrible, it is better to look it in the eye. I have always felt it's better to know than to not know because atleast then, you can do something about it.'

Savannah was silent, turning the thought over in her

mind. 'But, what if you can't do anything about it?' she asked eventually. 'Wouldn't it be better to...to just not know?'

'In my life,' smiled Dr Berry, 'I am yet to find a situation that one could do absolutely nothing about. One can always find something that helps, even if it is purely symbolic.'

'But, what if that doesn't change anything? Why waste the effort?'

'We put in the effort only if we actually believe that the principle is important enough.

Because that effort just might change something, someday,' laughed Dr Berry in return. 'There are no guarantees in life, my dear, except, of course, dying. And, even that need not be such a traumatic experience. However...'

'That doesn't seem enough,' she said, before falling silent. Savannah was still frowning, but where there might have been anger, there was now a fierce, argumentative light in her eyes.

'However,' smiled Dr Berry, 'as you say, sometimes, that is not enough. In those situations, I find it helps to...look at the situation anew. Take, for example, your diary. Since it is your own, I will not insult you by asking if you are familiar with the entries, but I will ask you, since you have been thinking about it from the time you first left it in my care: Did you note any pattern while you wrote it?'

'Pattern?' asked Savannah in surprise. 'What pattern? I don't understand, Dr Berry.'

'Observe,' smiled Rama Berry, taking the diary from her

lap and holding it open. Savannah could see how much age had thinned Dr Berry's skin, which seemed crinkled like parchment, especially around the nails.

'In the beginning,' Rama Berry flicked through the first few entries, 'your entries are very personal. They remain so, broadly speaking, until you begin to tell stories—stories that may have been inspired by real events.' The old doctor's finger tapped against the entry about the airplane. 'Moving forward,' she began to flick through the pages once more, 'the characters in your story grow, both in numbers and in importance.'

Savannah nodded, leaning forward to take the diary from Dr Berry. 'I never thought of reading my own work like that,' she thought, flipping through the diary.

'However,' Dr Berry's tone was contemplative, 'there is one common streak to almost all the entries in the diary, my dear.'

Savannah looked up, almost expecting to see a look of grim judgement on the diminutive doctor's face. Instead, Dr Berry wore a troubled frown, as though she was about to tell the story of a close friend who was going through a difficult period.

'My dear,' she leaned forward, patting Savannah's hand with her own, 'why do you carry so much sadness? Why do you always end your stories with a…with a jolt? Why must they all end with a jarring thump?'

'Because life's like that,' replied Savannah after a long, contemplative moment.

Her eyes, despite her best efforts, were already filling with tears. Her mood had been soaring a moment ago because she had never shown her diary to anyone before, and Dr Berry's praise had been as welcome as rain in the desert. But—just as her own stories did—Rama Berry's question had brought Savannah's thoughts back to earth with a sudden, emotion-rattling thump.

'That's because of the world we live in, doctor. We live in a world where people are killed in their sleep. Where a woman crying in a hospital, waiting to be attended to is asked to keep quiet and wipe her blood off the floor because the nurse feels miscarriages are no big deal. Where people are not willing to help an injured person in a car crash because they don't want to get involved in the police case afterwards.

We live in a world where people are willing to sell their perfectly viable organs in exchange of the latest iPhone. Where a friend refuses to acknowledge a friend just because she wasn't dressed up to the "standard".

Where buying birthday presents has become a formality. We don't buy something because it reminds us of someone; we buy it because it's of the same value of something that they bought us.

Where a father doesn't hesitate before pointing a gun at

his own child just because he is in love with someone who comes from different religious beliefs.

We live in a world where our egos, our issues keep us from complimenting other people. Where they keep us from loving the ones we love. Where limited editions trump greeting cards. Where practicality matters more than emotions. Where people care so much about what other people think that they have stopped living their own lives.

My question remains unanswered: Do we like who we have become?'

'There's no point,' Savannah sighed wearily, a moment later, tears sliding down her cheeks. 'There's no point in doing anything.'

Then, she put her head down and wept.

Sometime later—or perhaps it was much later—Savannah's tears dried, and she could once again speak.

'Even the writing...' she began tremulously, dabbing at her eyes, 'I don't even know how and why I began to write in the first place...'

'Because it was a way to vent and because it helped,' said Rama Berry firmly, letting go of Savannah's hand. 'It was necessary.'

Savannah offered the doctor a weak smile, still caught up in the whirlwind of emotions. I barely know this woman, the thought was faint and far in the background, but I do like her.

'More so,' smiled Dr Berry, 'my dear, you should continue

to write. I believe you mentioned, when you first came to see me, that you… I beg your pardon,' her smile turned mischievous, 'that your sister Sairah was working on a book?'

'Ah…' Savannah looked up offering a faint smile in return. 'Yes, doctor, I… I mean, no doctor. I was working on a book, but that was some time ago, and I guess I got stuck, so I stopped.'

'That's quite normal,' replied Dr Berry. 'But do finish it, my dear, if only for yourself.'

'But who will read it?' asked Savannah, her own smile growing slightly. 'I mean, you only read my diary because I'm your…'

Rama Berry chuckled and nodded. 'It is a sad fact, my dear, that few people read these days, especially fiction. However, there are many other ways to write, if you wish to be read. Have you ever considered writing for a publication of some kind?'

'Publication? Like a newspaper?' asked Savannah with an awkward laugh. 'I don't think I could. I…'

'Not only the newspaper, my dear. You could write anywhere. You could start a blog or you could write on the Internet somewhere—there are so many forms of social media these days. I do not doubt you would find people who would be happy to read your work and engage with your ideas. Think about it.'

'How will this help?'

'You will get to vent out about all the things and situations that make you unhappy and your readers might just learn something from your writing. You might be able to bring about a change. After all, good writing holds power, don't you think?'

'Yes, but,' frowned Savannah.

These are…these are my inner thoughts, she thought, how could I share them with perfect strangers?

'What is the matter, my dear?' asked Rama Berry. 'You do not seem pleased.'

'What if…' began Savannah hesitantly. 'What if people don't understand what I'm writing? What if I make a mistake?'

'Everybody makes mistakes,' smiled Dr Berry. 'If you want, I could introduce you to a few people who could help you begin. A distant relative of mine occasionally contributes to a small magazine, though it is only published online. I understand that one can even write for them anonymously, if one so wishes.'

'I… I…' Savannah paused, her emotions in a whirl once more. 'Maybe I could try…'

'Excellent,' smiled Rama Berry, standing up and walking gracefully to her desk. An imposing stack of forms, stapled together with a heavy clip, loomed ponderously on one corner. Lifting it up with only a slight grunt of effort, Dr Berry walked back to the couch, taking a seat next to Savannah once more.

'Now since that is settled,' her smile was bright, if a bit forced, 'as I mentioned in our last meeting, there are a lot of questionnaires to go through, before we can build a comprehensive psychological profile. I hope you came prepared, because if we don't get through these today, you'll have to wait another two weeks at least to finish them. I generally don't see patients this soon after first meeting them, but...' her voice trailed off into a mutter as she began to rustle through the forms on her lap.

'Ah,' she nodded, dragging a sheet of paper out of the middle of the stack. 'Alright, my dear. First question. What is your full name, your date of birth, and is this the first time you're assessing your mental health?'

Chapter Twenty-Seven

DEAD PEOPLE'S SOCIETY

Something happened today. I don't know if it's good or not, but something happened today.

I'd just woken up, and was having my morning cup of tea, when I got a text message from Dr Berry. 'Chk eml, hv wrk fr u. Tx, wl cl l8r.'

She's a genius, but I don't think she really understands that we don't need to use short words in text messages anymore.

Nevertheless, I checked my email and it turned out that Dr Berry had sent some of my work to someone to read. And they liked them!

Now, they want me to write for their magazine—it's published online—and like Dr Berry said, they're willing to let me do it anonymously. And, they're ready to pay me as well! There's just one catch—I have to write about a 'trending topic'.

What should I do?

~

I'm still not sure if I want to be published, but here's my first attempt at a magazine article. It's not really a 'trending topic', but I don't know what that is and that's the long and short of it.

FOR THE MAGAZINE
DEAD PEOPLE'S SOCIETY

The term 'ladies and gentlemen' is now officially defunct, because both ladylike women and gentlemanly men are now characters most likely in the grave.

A lady was someone who had class, style and grace. A gentleman was above all, courteous, dignified and broad-minded. What's common to both of these descriptions is that they're entirely dependent on people who agreed and followed the meaning of those adjectives, and that, above all, is the reason for this double homicide.

There will always be men who know and respect what it means to be a man. Men of that kind know that it's not about opening doors and carrying women across puddles. It's about loving and respecting women. By the same token, there will always be women who were born to be ladies; stylish in the absence of money, classy simply because they respect themselves, and graceful because they know that their beauty is meant for the world, and not for the mirror. On the other side, however, are the dedicated narcissists and the egotists, people who are too certain of their self-serving beliefs, no matter what the consequences are for other people. There is also another unusual kind—people who figure out their own realities, who stick to their own moral codes regardless or perhaps because of what life does to them.

The vast majority of people, however, are those who are still figuring out what their life is all about, people who are, as yet, not ready to claim a niche and stick to it. People who are still growing, yet required to act grown up. People who are more reactionary than principled. Advertisers routinely take advantage of this; almost every single ad on TV these days attempts to define what it means to be a man or a woman. While ads are a small part of everyday life and are not to be taken too literally, they're still very relevant to social beliefs—both as a description and a projection of the kind of people we are.

At the end of the day, however, it's not about public

opinion or what the TV tells us to believe. It's more about things that are talked about in public spaces, and values that we share as people. Chivalry is dead, but only the kind of chivalry that treats women like beautifully fragile possessions. Ladies are history too, but only the kind of ladies who need gentlemen to survive. What we have seen now is a redefinition of masculine and feminine roles—and the only thing for sure is that nobody's sure what makes a gentleman, and what isn't proper for a lady.

In all this uncertainty, a few things have become rock solid. Men and women are fundamentally different—in their biology, in the kind of wiring of their brains, in the ways their bodies evolve in their lifetimes, in the roles that society will expect them to play. There are some traits that are masculine and some that are feminine—and oddly, it's impossible to find a man with only masculine traits, or a woman with exclusively feminine ones. The ancient idea of gentility, that a man had a responsibility to protect and care for (and therefore had some rights over) the weaker woman, emerged from centuries of living in a world where physical strength was the defining characteristic—and men in this respect are fundamentally stronger. These days, the threats that people and families face are more abstract; and in this, it's more likely that on an average, women are the fundamentally stronger ones—mostly because women's brains are wired better to deal with different kinds of information at the same time.

While the world makes up its mind on the new-age lady and gentleman, there are some questions that are fairly relevant. Is mutual respect on the cards? How about accepting that men are superior in some spheres, and women in others? What about the joy a man feels when he knows he's taking care of his wife and kids? What if a woman finds the same joy in taking care of her husband and kids? Should the men of this century pay the price for the heavy-handedness of long-dead patriarchs, and accept the ornamental positions that women were relegated to? When will people understand that the concept of 'Feminism' that women are fighting for stands for equality of the sexes and not the superiority of women over men?

The only gentleman that's dead, and the only chivalry that's faded, is the one that existed to show-off how 'masculine' a man is. Men who respect women and behave lovingly towards them will do so whether there's a social advantage to it or not; and women who honestly respect themselves will always have men to love them. The connotations of what it means to be a 'gentleman' and a 'lady' have changed and to my mind, only the fundamental tenets of love, respect and equality is what should differentiate a gentleman from men and a lady from women.

~

Something terrible just happened.

After writing my article, I decided to step out and do some shopping. I was on my way home, when I saw something that set my blood on fire.

The fact that I couldn't do anything about it—I still can't do anything about it—just makes everything much more awful.

We were stuck in traffic at some signal, I don't even remember which, and everything was moving slowly. There was a gap in the traffic towards the left, just past a bus. My driver was trying to ease the car into that lane, but there wasn't much space to move.

Just then, this...this white blur rushed past the window, and there was this awful honking.

Some idiot, driving a bright white Ambassador, was moving through the traffic at a ridiculous speed, and had almost hit us as he overtook the bus. What that driver was doing was dangerous, and not to mention, utterly stupid. And, then the inevitable happened. A few hundred feet ahead, he crashed straight into the back of a Tempo.

Ordinarily, one would expect the driver of the Ambassador to not acknowledge his mistake, but instead get out, and indulge in a shouting match with the Tempo driver, after which he would conveniently escape before the cops could arrive to make life difficult for everyone in the area.

But, not this time.

This time, four large bearded men got out of the Ambassador, marched up to the driver of the Tempo, and started beating him to a pulp, without uttering a single word.

I was about to open my window, thinking I could help the driver in some way, before I looked around. Nobody on the street had moved. Since nobody looked like they were going to do anything—and I'm a five-and-a-quarter-foot tall woman—I got scared.

So, I stopped.

The Tempo driver, quite obviously, didn't stand a chance. He already looked like the kind of person who's been starving for the past few months—a discoloured shirt hanging loosely from his shoulders, sunken face to boot. And no matter how much he protested, begged for help, or begged them to stop—I can still hear him shouting, 'Kya kiya maine? Kyon maar rahe ho?' (What did I do? Why are you beating me?)—the pulping continued.

I asked my driver to get down and help, but neither did he get down, nor did he let me. I watched for a few seconds, feeling helpless and then I called the cops.

I felt sick. This was the first time I've ever been ashamed to say that I'm from this city.

This incident left me feeling so righteously angry at the world and my own impotence in this matter. For everybody else, it was just another incident in the big city, except, of course, for that Tempo driver who was lying on the side of the road, broken and bleeding.

To you, the Tempo driver, I make one promise.

I will write everyday, about something that happened in the city. You will be my conscience, and the conscience of whoever takes your story to heart.

Chapter Twenty-Eight

LOOKING FORWARD

So, my article was published...and they want me to write more.

But, they didn't care!

I could tell. They sent me an email, a few days ago. It was full of official sounding compliments—your articles generated a lot of page views, we're very happy to begin our collaboration, etc.—but, they don't actually care, not about the Tempo driver. Not really, at any rate. I looked it up on the website. It was filed under some section called 'Events in the City'.

Event? He's probably dead!

Dr Berry says I need to let go. Of course, she didn't come out and say it, but she went on and on about my needing to 'find an appropriate outlet to process these emotions'. And, she keeps harping on about that 'book deal' I made up. I can't tell her it never existed, so I'm going to have to find a publisher now. She was insistent that I 'build on the momentum', whatever that means.

Where am I ever going to find a publisher?

~

A Few Weeks Later:

So, I found a publisher.

At least, I found out how a lot of writers go about publishing their work. A friend of Aman's sister is an editor in a publishing house and she suggested I go to one of the literature festivals—or 'Lit Fests' as they call them—which keep taking place every few months in different parts of the country. Apparently, everyone goes to them to get an idea of how these things work. It seems so obvious, now that I know about it. There's a big one, next month, not too far away. And, I haven't been out of the city in a while so this would be my much-needed break!

I've met Dr Berry twice since the article got published. Last time, I asked her if she could prescribe something to help me sleep, but she refused, after asking me a whole bunch of questions that had nothing to do with anything. I mean how does it matter if I drink coffee after ten at night? She thought I needed to get out more, and to exercise; so, I have started going to the park again. I don't enjoy walking in this extreme cold weather but it makes me tired, so that's good. I'll probably sleep well tonight.

I should really book my tickets and hotel now. Aman said it's best done early.

~

Jaipur Lit Fest is only a fortnight away. I'm so nervous... but I'm also excited. I've been in the city for too long. Dr Berry was right; I do need to get out more.

But, I've also been writing.

Booking my ticket to Jaipur made me think...it would really be great to have something to show an editor if they ask what my book is about.

Note: Is it the editor who signs your book? Or is it someone else? I should ask Aman.

So, I now know for a fact that I don't want to write newsy stuff. I wrote a few more articles for that website, and they liked those too, but they keep burying my stories at the bottom of the contents page.

That said, writing a book is hard.

I still don't know what it's going to be about, but Dr Berry did suggest that I make it fictional. She said it would be easier in the long run. And that if I got stuck, I should just take an 'event', and begin from there.

'Put all your diary entries together, let the world read a little bit about themselves', she had said once. At first, I thought she might have been making fun of me, but she looked very earnest and I took her suggestion seriously.

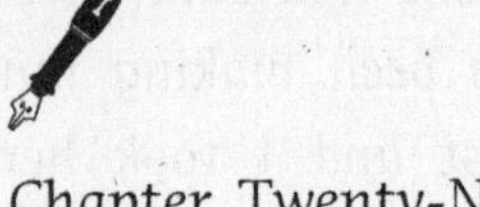

Chapter Twenty-Nine

JAIPUR LITERATURE FESTIVAL

Jaipur was AMAZING. There were so many people there!

I was so happy to meet like-minded people who liked to read and think. When I looked up the schedule before going for the festival, everything sounded so... overly intellectual. Sessions on Feminism, discussions about race and caste and money and power.

Book launches, film screenings, biographies, educational publishing, it was a long list of back-to-back events.

I didn't think I'd enjoy them at all. But, I ended up spending at least eight hours at the sessions every single day, and I wasn't even tired at the end. Though I didn't agree with everything I heard, or everyone I met.

During one of the sessions, the speaker started by asking everyone how they had travelled to the festival.

Many people said 'car', or 'train'. A few, like me, said 'airplane'. He got really nasty after that; he asked the people who said 'plane' if they realized 'how unbelievably privileged' we were. I really didn't like that. I thought that he was just mocking us for having money. I'm still not sure what he meant, but it did get me thinking.

He then asked how many of us were 'artists'. I raised my hand—like everyone else there—but then, I wished I hadn't. He asked how often we wrote about 'other people's problems'. I didn't understand at first, and for a while, it only got more confusing. He then asked, 'How many of you artists have genuinely tried to feel another's pain? To write as though that pain was your own? Without including your own biases, your own issues, your own perspective?'

I was so drawn into the conversation that I surprised even myself; I found myself raising my hand and replying that I did try to write about other people's pain but there might be traces of my own bias at times. That if I was completely objective, I either wouldn't write at all, or that I'd write textbooks.

A lot of people laughed, but the speaker wasn't happy.

The story he then told us has stayed with me, even though it's been a few days since I got back.

'I, myself, am from a rich family,' he said. 'I could

have joined the family business, and I did, for a while. I was managing one of the factories, and I spent about ten hours a day, thirty days a month doing that. I was earning well, too—enough that I could buy a fancy car after six months, and an even fancier apartment after a year, without taking any kind of loan. I truly did believe that I deserved that money. After all, many of my friends who went into banking or law were making as much as me, and working fewer hours.

But then, one day, after a long day at work, when I left for home, my car broke down, and I was stranded at the factory.

Worse, it was raining, and my clothes had gotten soaked while I was trying to get my car to start. The floor manager gave me a set of overalls, and after changing, I went to the factory's canteen to get a cup of coffee. I was pretty irritated; I'd already been at work for twelve hours on that particular day and it was most likely going to become fifteen. I was feeling quite out of place too. I have always felt uncomfortable about being so much richer than my workers, but like everyone always said, this is how the world works. There are winners, and there are losers, and it's a personal choice for everyone which group they want to be in. And I really didn't want to be in any other group, despite how uncomfortable my wealth made me feel.

That said, I really did feel uncomfortable that day at the canteen. Like an outsider who didn't fit in. If it wasn't for the fact that I was wearing worker's overalls, I doubt that people would have even left me alone—and I really didn't want to deal with low-level managers taking advantage and coming over to talk to me about this or that complaint. So, as soon as I got my coffee, I found a corner table and sat down, facing away from everyone else.

That's when I heard two foremen talking at a nearby table. They were complaining. They'd been working overtime, and had just finished a 10-hour shift. I felt quite happy hearing that. If I worked longer than my own workers, clearly I had no reason to feel out of place just because I earned more than them. I owned the company—or at least, my family did—and so, we deserved the profit. After all, we created jobs, and worked hard as well. People who complained about a 10-hour shift clearly didn't deserve to earn as much as I did; after all, I'd never complained.

I finished my coffee and left, deciding to go back to my office and wait there. On the way, I ran into one of my managers, one of the men who'd been supervising the day's shift. Out of curiosity, I asked how much the workers were getting paid. He looked surprised, but told me that they were contract labour, paid on a daily basis. Something like ₹150 per day.

I felt sick. That's merely ₹4,500 in a good month, that's how much I make every hour, 10 hours a day. And my job is behind the desk; theirs is total physical, hard work. And the fact that I'd never before thought to compare my salary with those who worked for me made it even worse.'

That night, when I got back to my hotel, I sat to jot down my daily expenses and suddenly everything seemed so unfair. I was paying almost ₹6,000 a night for the room I was staying in. Even the flight that I took to Jaipur had cost several thousand.

The next morning, though, I woke up more cheerful than I had in months because something good did come out of the whole experience. I suddenly realized, in between tears, that there are people who suffer through far more difficult lives than I do. That even if I feel alone, and lonely, and even if the world I live in is filled with selfish, greedy people who don't give two hoots about anyone but themselves...at least I don't have to struggle everyday just to put food on the table.

Every morning when I wake up, I have a roof above my head, warm water in my shower, food on my table and my family and friends who love me.

Maybe Dr Berry was right. Maybe some of the

problems in my life are only there because I don't value how much I do have.

~

At the Literature Festival, I did manage to meet a few publishers. Junior editors, mostly, but I did get some phone numbers and email addresses. There was one rather lovely girl—actually, come to think of it, she can't be more than a few years older than me—who really seemed interested in my writing.

I emailed her some of my work the other day, and she replied this morning saying that she was really interested in seeing more of my work. She also said that she enjoyed the 'honesty' in my writing. I'm not sure what she meant, but I thought that if it was working, I should keep going. And so, I did.

Chapter Thirty

AT THE LIBRARY

Two weeks had passed since the Lit Fest. I had called Dr Berry quite a few times but her assistant told me she was out of town for some seminar and won't be back until the end of the month. I took a chance and messaged her on her phone requesting her to meet me as soon as she got back. There was no reason in particular except, I had gotten used to seeing her from time to time. It just felt like something I had to do. Like how you bow your head without thinking every time you pass by a place of worship. It felt like she was guiding me through life, carefully. Like if I ran things past her, they would be fine.

It was a Tuesday, sometime around noon; I was still in my pyjamas, contemplating whether or not to wash my hair, when I received a text from Dr Berry.

'Hi! Not in town. B bck tmrw. Meet @ British Libry.

Thursdy, 4pm. C u.'

Her age could be revealed in her messages very clearly. Her use of punctuation in her messages showed how new she was to today's technology.

On Thursday, I reached the British Library before time, eagerly waiting for Dr Berry to arrive. This was the first time we were going to meet outside the walls of a hospital. It felt good for a change but also a little weird; I was a little nervous about it not being just us. There wasn't a couch today, neither the privacy of her room. But, being a library, it was still quiet and peaceful, and not new to me. I went and sat in my favourite spot and saved a seat for Dr Berry. Moments later, she arrived. She was wearing a 'Visitors Pass' around her neck. In her left hand, she carried a black purse with a green water bottle popping out. I waved my hand at her, hoping to grab her attention, but when she didn't look, I stood up and made a 'Psssssssssss' sound. Finally, she looked in my direction and started walking towards the empty chair next to me.

'Here, take this!' she whispered, handing over a few A4 sheets to me.

'I'll take an hour may be, make sure you fill this in,' saying that she began to walk away towards the bookshelves.

Another set of questionnaire, I thought at first, feeling irritated. But, on looking closely, I realized, that the pages were blank, front and back. I was confused and started flipping through them again when I saw just one word written at the beginning: Childhood.

I got up and went in the direction of the bookshelves, not knowing what to do, when I saw Dr Berry's face buried in books.

'Doctor!' I called out.

'Hush!' she shushed me and without looking in my direction, she handed me a pen and whispered, 'Write about it, whatever comes to your mind.'

I stood there for a few minutes, feeling like a fifth grader with an assignment at hand. I then turned around and walked straight to my spot and began writing.

CHILDHOOD

When Mom taught us ABC
She also taught us how to be
We were told to be nice
Even when we weren't feeling so good inside
She asked us to be polite
Even if it meant to swallow our pride
Hurting someone was the biggest sin
So, without using our brain, we wore a silly grin
And then, there were talks About 'expressing yourself'
So, choosing the right words, became a task
You couldn't buy for pelf

But, with the passing time
All I can do is sit and whine
All that I have learnt by far
Seems to have gone down the drain
For I have been hurt
And there is no refrain
Have people lost the insight to tell right from wrong?
Shouldn't they be reminded of the good old song?
When dessert was the only thing that was considered to be kept cold
When eyes could express feelings and memories were not sold!

I was asked to practise 'writing' at home, once I was done with my homework in order to have a better handwriting.

There were plenty of half-filled Cursive Handwriting books, in the study; I remember this one particular book.

It was a Moral Science book with additional space to practise writing.

It had all possible supposedly-moral quotes that a 7-year-old could read but not necessarily understand.

The reason I remember all this is because being the hoarder I am, I still have my stuff from back then lying around somewhere in the study.

And it was only a few days ago, that I went through some of it.
The first page read:
WHEN THE GOING GETS TOUGH
THE TOUGH GET GOING.
I wrote that phrase over and over again
With every line I saw the improvement in the way I wrote it, but
I guess that's all I did
My eyes followed the tip of my pencil
Not once did I pay attention to the words that tried so hard to speak to me
I get it now
And I need to be reminded again and again
To get through the day
Don't you too?

When situations play hard on you, you play harder
That's my way to look at it
I don't know if it still is
But I'm quite sure it was...

When dad passed away
I didn't shed a tear
I didn't want Mom to see her 10-year-old cry
I pretended like it was all okay!
I was being tough

I was playing harder
But was I supposed to?
I was 10
I could have behaved my age
I could have cried in that room full of crying people
But I didn't
I didn't want to seem weak
I was strong
I was strong for my mum
But I still remember hearing a whisper in that room full of unpleasant sounds
I heard her look at me and say to another
'She just doesn't care!'
I got up and ran inside...straight to the bathroom
I looked into the mirror
My eyes picked up a shade of red.
That was the first time
I felt the need to send this question out in the void
How could anyone be so harsh to a 10-year-old?
How could they doubt the love of a daughter for her most favourite person in the world?
How could they not see?
I was holding it
I was holding it deep down
Trying so hard to keep it in
It made my stomach churn

And here I am
All these years later
Still questioning
Insensitivity and shallowness

That sentence
That soft voice carrying the harshest of words
Changed me
Changed my existence

I still sit down in the quiet
And ask myself
Had I not heard those words,
Would I still be the same person?
Had she not judged a 10-year-old,
Would I have lived differently?

'Perhaps,'
I say to myself
I would have hugged Mum and I would have told her,
That even though I spent just 10 years of my life with dad
I still try to revisit those memories, every chance I get.

The world is cruel
It's tough

They rip us apart, every chance they get
All we do is survive!

It was an hour or so later, when I stopped writing. I looked over and realized Dr Berry's hand was on my shoulder. As I put the cap back on the pen, she picked up the sheets and said, 'I'm sorry, I have to go now, but come see me tomorrow at the hospital, same time.' Saying just that, she left, taking what felt like an examination answer sheet, with her.

I couldn't tell if I was feeling better before writing that stuff about my childhood or after. In that moment, I was just feeling things. I sat still for another hour or so just by myself. I didn't feel like looking around or talking to anyone. I didn't even feel like pulling out a book and reading. My gaze was fixed on my fingertips. There were blue ink marks everywhere.

Chapter Thirty-One

THE LAST SESSION

'Is she inside?' I asked the assistant. 'Can I go now?' I asked almost immediately.

'Wait Savannah!' she said at once and handed me an envelope.

'What's this?' I asked.

'The doctor didn't come in today, but she sent this for you. Here, take it. We will reschedule for some other day. Sorry about the inconvenience!'

The doctor's assistant, Mena, said those lines like she had rehearsed them. Like it was okay to call someone and not show up.

'What? How come?' I asked, half confused, half surprised at Dr Berry's behaviour. I met her after almost a month at the library yesterday, we barely spoke a few words to each other and then she asked me to come today and all I got was an envelope.

'But, it was she who asked me to come today, where is she?' I coaxed.

'She had to attend a wedding. She would be coming in a little later, or she may not come at all today. Nothing is certain. She said she'd call.'

I came out of the room because Mena looked like she was in a hurry to lock the room and leave since there was nobody but me and I too had been served, so her job for the day was done!

I had sent my driver to the dry cleaners' thinking I would take at least an hour in the session, but here I was, with nothing to do so I decided to go to the cafeteria downstairs.

'One cappuccino, please!' I ordered and then I opened the envelope.

Hi Savannah!

I have never done this before.

Writing to a patient. Well, I don't even want to address you as that.

You are not a patient.

You are a beautiful young girl with a beautiful heart who has her whole life ahead of her.

It hurts me to see someone as young as you be so angry at your life and the lives around you.

I try to refine and reframe my methods for each individual who comes to see me. You see, I have always been a fan of Montessori training. I believe that no two people in this world are alike, so why should they be treated in the same manner?

Some like the colour blue, some find it depressing, some like cherries, the seeds of which annoy others. Take the number thirteen, considered unlucky by most, except for the people born on the 13th who think otherwise.

We all are different from each other.

With you, being such a good writer yourself, I thought what could be better than writing this last session down. After all, written words have more credibility and I'm sure YOU of all people would agree with me.

The concept of birth and rebirth is still a mystery to man. Whether or not our souls come back after we die is still unknown. And even if we do, we come back as humans or take another form is an even bigger question that remains unanswered.

All these unanswered questions arouse curiosity and just for the amusement of it alone, once in a while, whenever I get a chance, I pick up books on such subjects.

It was this one time that I came across an

exceptionally well-written book by a doctor in the States, in which he discussed this particular topic at length. He talked about taking rebirth in groups. To put it in simple words, it means that our immediate family, our friends, people we know, people who cross our path, we all have somehow known each other in our past lives. It is not necessary that we share the same kind of relationship with them like we did in our past lives, like my sister in this life could've been my mother in the previous lifetime or my best friend could've been my husband in another life. But somehow, we were all connected then and that's the reason we are still connected. We have unfinished business which is why we keep coming back.

In my line of work, there is so much to learn everyday; reading is a big part of moving forward. Whether it is a case history or research work, journals or articles, reading is a big part of my life. But, it is only once in a while that you read something that stays with you forever. Well this was that!

When I first met you, you were lost and broken. I'm not sure if someone has the power to fix what is broken but one can only try. But in the process of trying to make you feel better Savannah, I have learnt a lot from you!

Your soul is pure and intact. Unharmed, untouched by the shallow. I feel like you are one of my own, like I know you from before. But having said that, I would also like to say that yes, this is going to be the last time for us.

There is a fine line between getting attached and getting addicted. I don't want someone as young and bright as you to depend on a psychiatrist. You are capable of achieving anything you aspire for and you don't need me or anyone like me for that.

So now, read this carefully. Repeatedly, if required.

After visiting a page from your childhood yesterday, I felt there is still a lot of negativity, hurt and sadness.

I'm not saying you haven't gotten better. I mean look at yourself, from being a quiet person, mostly stuck in a corner, writing away in your diary, you have become someone who now writes for a living.

A few months ago, when I first met you, you thought your writing was making you weak. You thought if you went on writing about the events and episodes around you, you wouldn't be able to be normal. It was consuming you, and I agree.

But, look how far you have come in no time; how much you have accomplished. You will soon be a published writer. An author of a book in her twenties. Isn't that an achievement?

And, you could do all this just by converting what you thought was making you weak into your biggest strength.

I am very proud of you, my dear!

Remember, a person feels insecure if she's in an environment that doesn't suit her. A person feels insecure if she's behaving in a way alien to her true nature. Put someone in a hostile environment and then force her to put up a facade to get on with her life, and you've killed her right there.

I know a guy who's been through something like that—or at least, that's what he claims. He says that right from the beginning, he had to pretend to be someone he wasn't, just so that people would leave him alone long enough for him to maintain some measure of sanity. When I asked him for more details, he began to shout. Fair enough, there's something disturbing him for sure. However, isn't that something everyone goes through in life? Every single person has been through some sort of pain. You never really grow until something bad happens to you, since that's what gets you thinking in the first place.

Coming back to you Savvy, I've got a theory on

this. I think it'll be good for you. Trust me on this one, like you have in the past. It'll be okay, I promise.

I think, in all honesty, that you don't really consider yourself worth very much, which is why you have to come up with all these complex excuses to avoid looking the truth in the face. Fair enough, your childhood was painful. It must have been really difficult, not having someone to pour your heart out to. Everyone needs someone to lean on, and not being able to trust anyone long enough to take a bit of weight off of your shoulders is a harsh way to grow up.

But consider this, you are who you are for the simple reason that you went through all of that in the past. Yes, it left you with a bunch of scars, and I doubt that you'll ever be free of all your demons. Look at what that gave you though. You know more about yourself right now than most people ever will—and that's something.

You've experienced cruelty first-hand, so you know not to be cruel yourself—your scars are a product of that, and I doubt you'd want to give this sort of grief to anyone else.

Fine, you don't trust people, which is a big, big disadvantage when it comes to rebuilding your life, but you've already burned yourself in the fire of your own personal hell for so long that most of your insecurities are already gone.

You were forced to think about yourself and your life at an age when only a few people even know the concept of who they are—and you've been doing that for so long that you've even begun to understand the deeper meaning of life.

I could go on with this forever and I know that as soon as I say something, you'll have a comeback, something to bring us back to the starting point. There's no point in arguing on this—this is about you, only you.

Stop beating yourself up.

You're fine, you really are.

You just need to start believing in yourself and the people around you a little more.

The world is not as evil as you think it is.

I am surprised how you still haven't noticed the most obvious thing.

All your answers lie within your own diary.

You complain about the ill that happens to others, but not once were you glad that it didn't happen to you. It's one thing to understand someone's pain but it is a totally different thing when you start feeling that pain.

Understand, my dear, that there is a difference

between sympathy and empathy. Have you once thanked the Almighty for what he has made out of your life?

You asked this once yourself, in one of your diary entries; something about our sufferings being related to our karma. Aren't you glad that your karma is not as heavy as the ones around you?

Isn't it a good thing that you have been doing so well as a human that you have so far been saved from all the ugliness around? You want to change the world? You can. We all can, in our own way. But, you wouldn't be able to do it by borrowing sadness. Lend a smile instead.

If you see someone unhappy, make them happy; don't bring their sadness into your life.

I remember singing this prayer at our school assembly back when I was a kid, I don't remember all the words, but just a few lines,

Make me a channel of your peace
where there is hatred let me bring love
where there is injury, your pardon Lord

Oh, Master grant that I may never seek
So much to be consoled as to console
to be understood as to understand
To be loved as to love with all my soul...

Like I said, we never forget some things!

The only way for someone to live in a hostile environment and still be at peace is to realize that they make their own world. There's no need for facades, no reason to lie to yourself and to others. Just be YOU—it's what you were born to do.

A highly-enlightened person once told me, 'Our life is what we make of it.'

Imagine yourself standing in front of a wall. Now, if you choose to throw a black ball at the wall, it will bounce back and come back to you in the form of a black ball, but if you choose to throw a white ball at the same wall, it will bounce back and find way in your life in the form of a white ball. The question is which colour ball are you going to send out? What is it that you want in return?

White or black?

'White' I muttered, wiping my tears away.

Maybe she's right!

Maybe people aren't as cruel as I think they are.

Maybe it was time for me to forget what had happened and move on.

Too many maybe's were flooding my brain; I felt exhausted.

The letter had drained me out and my hot cappuccino

was only missing a cube of ice.

I folded it carefully, crease on crease and placed it in my bag. When I went up to the cash counter, to pay the bill, it suddenly dawned on me that my diary was still upstairs, in the doctor's room.

I wasn't sure if I was going to come back to this place anytime soon so I thought it would be a good idea to just take it with me right now.

I called the driver and asked him to meet me outside in ten minutes, I wasn't sure if the doctor's assistant would still be there.

So one more time, I walked towards the elevator, hoping for it to be my last. The doors opened in no time and for once there was nobody inside. I stepped in and turned around to face the door when I heard someone yell, 'Hold it!'

Within what felt like a fraction of a second, there were paramedics, doctors and people pushing the patient-gurney inside the elevator. I felt nervous to look at the patient so I looked down at my shoes, but there was blood everywhere. I covered my nose and mouth with my scarf and gathered some courage to look up when I realized, the people were not people, it was Mena, the assistant, holding a pair of sandals in her hand and the patient wasn't any patient, it was a tiny old lady, dressed in pink which was now red. It was Dr Berry. Dr Rama Berry. My Dr Berry. The one I came to meet.

It felt like my heart had stopped beating and as the

elevator's doors closed, it became harder to breathe. The doctors, the paramedics, they all were talking to each other, giving instructions on what should be done. One of them had his fingers pressing an exposed vein around her neck, her stomach was bleeding, and her insides were now visible on the outside. It made me queasy but throwing up was not an option, not at that minute, not in that elevator. Everything was happening so quickly in front of my eyes, I didn't know what to say or do. I was shocked and scared at the same time.

I looked at Mena meaning to ask her what happened, but in that moment all I could manage was a 'How?'

She grabbed my hand and hugged me tight. I could almost hear her heart pounding.

'It... It was a van... a white van... it was big.

I... no, We...

She called me... She said she's coming... She needed her keys.

We were very close to the hospital... on the pavement... we were standing there, I went inside the supermarket to... to... buy... water, she was thirsty, she only asked me to buy a bottle... "Room temperature, Mena", she shouted, she was thirsty and when I came back, they drove into her... she was hit in front of me... I saw it... I saw them driving into her and the many others who stood around her. And one by one, they all flew and fell into the other direction. The van... the white one, just kept speeding past. There... there was so much blood ... so many of them ... on the road ... bleeding ... lots of them but nobody helped. The shopkeepers ... they closed their shops ... the people needed help ... I dragged Dr Berry here. We were close by.'

It was difficult to believe what I had heard was true. Hearing her talk, I felt my stomach churn and it made me feel even more nauseated, but again throwing up was not an option, not at that time, not in that elevator.

'We need to hurry up, go bring her medical records,' shouted the doctor in Mena's direction while getting off the elevator at the 'OT' floor.

Few seconds passed, when the elevator door dinged open, Mena ran out and turned right.

'Fifth Floor' the automated voice must have said, only this time, I couldn't hear it.

All I could hear was Dr Berry's voice: 'The world is not as evil as you think it is!'

And in that elevator, at that moment, I gave up.

ACKNOWLEDGEMENTS

What started as a hobby has finally turned into something meaningful.

Thank you Ma, Meeta Godhwani, for living your life as an excellent example for your daughters.

A big thank you to my husband, Himanshu, for pushing me to finish what I kept putting off. You have no idea how much your love and support means to me.

Abhiraj and Rajveer, my babies, my heart bursts with joy every time I look at you two. Thank you for letting me sneak into my study to write this book. I can't thank God enough for making me your mom.

My gratitude to Mummy and Papa, Rajni and Ashok Lalwani, for providing their support always as one would do to a daughter and not a daughter-in-law. I feel blessed to have you both in my life.

Thank you to my elder sister, Shivina, for being my number one stylist and for patiently letting your photo gallery fill with my photographs.

A tight hug to Twinkle, my ray, for suffering through one hundred rounds of editing the raw manuscript. Who would have thought that your English training would be put to such good use?

Thank you Masi, Poonam Parwani, for helping me tap the spiritual side of me. Our long conversations help me grow as a person.

A shout-out to Lavish and Urvashi—my friends, family and the finest critics. The trim-size wouldn't have changed if it weren't for you two.

A big hug to Gunjan Ghai for casually asking one day, 'Why don't you write a book?' Thanks to you Chinku, I did!

Mr Shantanu Ray Chaudhuri, I cannot thank you enough for everything you taught me in the world of writing. I'm so glad that Jaten helped me get in touch with you. I hope someday I can inspire others as you have inspired me.

Thank you, Mr Kapish Mehra for your timely advice on the book and also the great team you have at Rupa Publications. A big hug to Yamini for having faith in my work.

I am immensely grateful to my entire family, for giving me so much love.

Last, and most importantly, I am grateful to the many people who saw me through this book and all those who put their faith in me by sharing their stories. I hope I have been able to portray the smallest fraction of emotion that you went through. I am sorry you had to go through it.